مرحلة النوم

Mohamed Kheir

translated from Arabic by
Robin Moger

SLEEP PHASE

TWO LINES
PRESS

Originally published as مرحلة النوم
© 2024 by al Kotob Khan Publishing & Distribution
Translation copyright © 2025 by Robin Moger

Two Lines Press
www.twolinespress.com

ISBN: 978-1-949641-78-3
Ebook ISBN: 978-1-949641-79-0

Cover design by Jonathan Pelham
Cover art: detail of *Goodbye My Homeland* by Hossam Dirar.
© Hossam Dirar, used by permission of the artist
Design by Sloane | Samuel
Printed in the United States of America

Library of Congress Cataloging-in-Publication Data

Names: Khayr, Muhammad, 1978- author. | Moger, Robin, translator.
Title: Sleep phase / Mohamed Kheir ; [translated by] Robin Moger.
Other titles: Marhalat al-nawm. English
Description: San Francisco, CA : Two Lines Press, 2025.
Identifiers: LCCN 2024052361 (print) | LCCN 2024052362 (ebook)
ISBN 9781949641783 (paperback) | ISBN 9781949641790 (ebook)
Subjects: LCGFT: Novels.
Classification: LCC PJ7942.H42 M3713 2025 (print) |
LCC PJ7942.H42 (ebook) | DDC 892.7/37--dc23/eng/20241214
LC record available at https://lccn.loc.gov/2024052361
LC ebook record available at https://lccn.loc.gov/2024052362

1 3 5 7 9 10 8 6 4 2

1

WARIF

It took him a while to realize that this was Talaat Harb Street. He wandered in under cover of red maple and broad-leaved walnut trees; high-crowned poplars were dressed in a single line like an honor guard, hiding the street's khedival facades from view. More than once he was startled by squirrels, darting through his legs as they scampered with their walnuts to the chestnut and pine woods, which occupied the site of the old stone pedestal and flagpole. Then the intersection, formerly a babel of car horns and the sputter bang of motorbikes short-cutting through lines of cars that yielded to the commands of rural conscripts, traffic signals made flesh. Where all that had once been, there were now only green tracks, grass flattened by feet that moved quietly between the trees and carpets of leaves that announced autumn's onset, the chatter of the sparrows and parakeets hopping between treetops, and a breeze freighted with a faint dampness, as though the morning's dew had been held suspended until this afternoon, through which Warif was walking in search of an address and marveling. It wasn't that the names of the streets and squares had changed, he told himself; they hadn't: it was that the streets and squares themselves were different and now seemed estranged from those names.

On his right, at the corner where formerly a line of Central Security trucks had stood in front of kiosks selling books and foreign-language newspapers, he saw a gym. The people inside, exposed by the plate-glass, were hammering away at their machines, running in place and staring out at the wooded square with eyes that were lost in their inner worlds. A little peculiar to be working out now, at midday, Warif thought. He remembered a trip he'd made long ago, alone, to a country in the north, where at night the windows of the municipal sports center lit up and he could step out of the bar where he drank and watch the girls running behind the glass, bursting with health, as invisible to them in that darkness as he was during the day.

He caught his reflection. He had forgotten what he looked like; from what he saw now, and what he could remember, he hadn't changed so much: still the almost-white-man skin, the fair hair that he shared with the pedestrians who surrounded him now, here, on this reborn street, this new age for neighborhood and country.

He turned toward Abdeen. On the lefthand side of the street, in place of the little shops where he used to buy light switches, lightbulbs, and mobile-phone accessories, stood a row of Asian restaurants; the dramatic reliefs of a Japanese restaurant's entrance had supplanted the driving school from which, one long-ago day, an aging and irritable instructor had emerged to teach Warif how to negotiate the chaotic and now-forgotten jams that plagued his test streets: Mansour, Mubtadiyan, and Qasr al-Ainy.

At the crosswalk coming into Bab al-Louq, he paused. It was impossible to tell whether the mechanical voice calling the signals was speaking a foreign-accented Arabic or some Egyptian-accented version of a foreign language; it was, in any case, clearly audible in the still quiet of the street, with the absence of honking vehicles and human cries. The battered steel fencing of the Bab al-Louq parking lot had been pulled down, and it was now studded with flowers and stands for pushbikes, while the sidewalks of the saucer-shaped square were dotted with coffeeshop tables, their mostly young customers drinking coffee and toying with pastries and cakes. Students, it looked like; Warif wondered what they could be doing here. None were old enough to be working, after all. Had the newcomers brought their children with them? It would make sense, he told himself, as he crossed the square with a gaggle of pedestrians. On Hoda Shaarawi Street he turned down a little alley whose wall bore a vast mural of an African-looking woman, a pop star perhaps, gazing at what seemed to be a tiny planet Earth. On the other side of the passageway, there was another picture: a queue of little men in identical blue suits, trudging submissively, listlessly, into the distance; by the time the wall ran out they still hadn't gotten to where they were going.

Emerging from the other end of the alley, Warif peered again at the address on his phone, then looked up. It had to be here, this big building where the state news agency used to stand. Gone were the long, yellow balconies; sheer glass walls now rose up into a skyscraper, and instead of the stairway up to the door, you now stepped directly from the street into reception. At a desk to the left of the entrance, a man with Indian features glanced at him inquiringly and Warif gave his name. The man checked something on his screen and told him to go up to the tenth floor. The lift was empty all the way up, then the door slid back and he emerged into a long corridor of closed doors. It was utterly silent. Tentatively, he walked down the corridor until, at the far end, there was a click, and a door opened to reveal a man of medium height and build and unplaceable ethnicity who said, in English, "Mr. Warif? Please come in."

The sun in the room was dazzling. The autumnal glow outside hadn't been half this strong, he thought. Instinctively, he looked about for some explanation other than the broad window that looked out over the double-row of gum acacias that lined either side of Sabri Abou Alam, the inverted pyramids of their crowns melding into a single green roof that once upon a time would have covered the smell of frying taamiya and the murmur of memorial services at the mosque next door to the Armenian-Catholic cathedral.

On the wall behind the man, now at his desk, there hung a reproduction of Mahmoud Saeed's *Bahri Girls*. The three women in the painting calmly observed Warif over the top of their gauzy veils. Well, two watched him; the third had her eyes closed. Compared to the space occupied by the women and the sky in whose far-left corner floated a cottony cloud shaped like a flat cap, the little wedge of sea seemed negligible, but it nevertheless touched something in Warif, called him back through the years to memories of that compound stink of iodine and grilled fish. He could almost see himself, that him of before, a skinny young man teetering along the top of the fat stone wall on the Alexandrian corniche, trying to catch the eyes of squawking girls…

The unplaceable man brought him back to the here-and-now, the office off Hoda Shaarawi:

"It's not often we receive a request like yours."

There was nothing to say to this, so Warif simply nodded and waited, listening to the voice that, he felt now, had the metallic edge of the traffic signal.

"The fact is, most people are quite satisfied with the current state of affairs. One might even venture to say happy."

What came to Warif's mind was the old adage about no two fingers on the same hand being alike, but what he said was, "There are always exceptions, though. As you know."

Despite his many years working as a translator, perhaps because of them, Warif had always felt that his English, with its agglomerations of movie dialogue and dictionary phrasing, made him into another person. With that experience in mind, he sensed that English was also not the first language of the man dealing with him now. That same ghost of quotation seemed to haunt the man's words, and, for a moment, it was as though the two strangers were both strangers to themselves as they faced each other beneath the painted gaze of the girls.

The man leafed through some pages (Warif was quite certain that he'd no need to check, that he was only pretending to read them), then in an almost lazy way, as if talking only to pass the time, he said, "And you would be one of these exceptional individuals?"

Warif understood this to be a reference to prison—or to what had led to prison, perhaps—but he only frowned. "Being exceptional was never my dream."

The man appeared not to have heard him.

"Warif Shaheen…not an especially common name in this country, I would've said. Or am I wrong about that?"

"My family's roots go back to the Levant."

Even as he said this, Warif was confident that the foreigner couldn't have come to such a conclusion on his own, and he realized that the information channels must still be functioning. An image flickered in his mind—his father, waving goodbye outside the university tram stop in Shatby—then blinked out. For the first time, he saw the man give the very faintest of smiles.

"In any case, your request shouldn't prove impossible."

The smile widened millimetrically.

"It seems you know people, Mr. Warif. Even this meeting would be beyond the reach of most."

Warif only nodded, doing his best not to think of Sally. The man straightened slightly in his chair and said, "You'll need to complete a few steps. We will send you a letter with the time and place of your next appointment and the documents you'll need. I don't promise anything, but I wish you luck."

The man stood but made no move to accompany Warif to the door, which clicked shut behind him as he left. He came back down the corridor with its impassive doors to find the lift waiting for him, open and empty. The Indian in reception was absorbed in his computer. On the street outside he briefly considered paying a visit to his old apartment on Adly Street, but a twinge in his back and a flutter in his left knee made him reconsider and he turned left instead. On the corner, just before the turn into Youssef al-Guindy, he encountered a flight of steps leading down and a sign over the entrance: *The Nile*. How had they managed to cut a tunnel through all those nineteenth-century foundations?

He hesitated, then tripped down the short flight of steps. He had been expecting graffiti and buskers but there was none of that: the tunnel was a long corridor, illuminated by what had to be concealed lighting. It reminded him of the effect in the office he'd just left. The walls were a mosaic panorama of the best-known examples of the city's khedival architecture, the very buildings he passed beneath; the floor was grass-green with a carpet's give and swallowed the sound of footsteps. And there were lots of them down here: Europeans strode purposefully back and forth. Their single-mindedness was infectious, and he quickened his pace to match them. Or was it that he feared being found out?

As it came to an end, the tunnel broadened, and at the head of the stairs he could see a sky filled with clouds, sisters to those in Mahmoud Saeed's painting. Even as he climbed, he knew what he would see and refused to believe it until there it was before him. The tunnel had indeed led him right to the Nile: beneath the woodland they'd made out of Tahrir and out onto the riverbank. Instead of chickpea carts there were palms, the short, tubby type with trunks like pineapples, and where the salesmen and women once circled with cakes, boiled eggs, and roses, there were chairs and benches, some of wood, some stone, scattered over the tongues of grass that sloped down to the water. People sat on and around them, singly and in groups, some playing instruments, mostly guitars, the rest smoking or drinking beer. He could make out bottles of Stella here and there and felt somehow reassured amid the babel of unfamiliar languages.

He looked out to the opposite bank, at the Gezira Tower and the Opera House's dome, as if to satisfy himself that he was still at home, when suddenly he sensed he was being watched. It was a talent he'd nurtured back in the old days, or say, one that had been built into him by fear and an instinct for survival. At last, through the huddles of noisily conversing youths, against the scarcely felt lapping of the Nile's small waves and those birdcalls that managed to punctuate the hubbub, he saw them: a pair of eyes, lazily observing him. Their owner was dressed in the uniform of a security guard, leaning against a motorbike that leaned in turn against a mound whose synthetic turf exactly matched the green of the lawns. Her hair, streaked blonde and brown, was pulled back into a bun and a pair of sunglasses hung at her chest. There was a little holster at her hip: a gun perhaps, or a taser. She shifted her gaze as an identically dressed man at her side whispered something in her ear, then smiled and resumed her casual scrutiny of Warif, flicking her gaze over him, as though unintentionally. Warif patted the wallet that still held the code for his recently concluded appointment, then his phone buzzed and he stiffened. The message was from Sally, asking if he was home yet. He tapped out a reply, replaced the phone in his pocket, and was looking back out over the Nile when suddenly it struck him that the painting in that unplaceable man's office might have been the original.

2

SALLY

She burst in, as though it was her place, not his, high heels making her even taller than she already was, and got straight to the point:

"So it's not hopeless after all. Congratulations!"

He was standing in what, since getting out, had become his favorite spot: halfway out onto the balcony with his back to the living room. He was looking over the forest that started north of the Magra al-Uyoun aqueduct and spread toward Downtown. It must have been planted and established with extraordinary speed and care. He more-or-less lived in this room now; the back of the apartment might as well have not existed: he'd bolted the windows and shut all the doors and was thinking that maybe he'd just board it all up. He didn't want to see or hear, let alone look at, the cafés and markets and street corners at the back. Fortunately for him, the apartment—his parents' before him—sat on the line that divided the two neighborhoods. Or should that be two time periods? But he still felt uneasy, as though without warning, while he slept perhaps, this place might be swallowed up entirely by the other. As if an earthquake had shifted things, say, and he would wake to find them all around him, surrounded by cigarette smoke, the clatter of dominos, the bus horns, and dance music. And their laughter. Their contented, happy, confident laughter; the laughter that was like a yawn; the laughter of shame-faced triumph, of a redundancy at once embarrassing and fortuitous. If he fell in with them, he'd never get out, and Sally, who had never been his to begin with, would leave him.

Yesterday, watching from his post at the balcony, he had noticed that a rank of construction vehicles had appeared, parked a few meters from the building. His heart had flipped. If he hadn't been standing as he was, propped against the doorframe, half-in and half-out of the living room, he would have crumpled to the floor. He knew they'd like nothing better than for a random piece of urban rezoning to definitively draw a line between the locals and the newcomers, their happy indolence finally sealed and complete, and he suddenly recalled a recurring dream that had visited him during the early years of his incarceration, once he'd adjusted to sleeping under the permanently burning lights. He'd dreamed that he was asleep at home when a group of burly men burst into his bedroom. He would wake, panicked, to find himself in the cell, and reassured that nothing could be worse than the situation he found himself in, would go back to sleep.

Sally called his name. She'd poured herself a glass of white wine and was sipping at it, long brown legs extended atop the arabesque coffee table that his father had bought from Bab al-Ghouriya back in the old days—escorting it home, with Warif's assistance, on the roof of an old wreck of a taxi. They'd sat at either end of the back seat, each reaching an arm through a window and gripping the table's edge as they kept an eye out for vans and buses and shouted warnings to motorcyclists and moped riders. Once home, his mother had checked it over. Though it was undamaged, she'd still complained, telling his father that the rim that framed the tabletop would make it impossible to clean, to which his father had accused her of being lazy. Warif had left the apartment before hearing her reply and had gone back to his own, the first place he had ever called his own, in the now-extinct network of alleyways once known as Maarouf.

In that extraordinary tone of voice she had, which somehow managed to combine self-confidence with equivocation, Sally was saying, "I expect that as soon as you get your first paycheck, you'll be able put it all behind you…"

Spoken as though she'd seen a hundred, nay a thousand, do exactly that: get their first check and forget. She wasn't looking at him, but, wine in hand, her head was gently nodding up and down. Maybe she was imagining him finally getting this job of his back, just like that, as she'd predicted; but then there was that lack of finality that often blunted her words, the way she drew out that "I expect," because she knew, just as that man in the office had divined that very morning, that exception's finger had marked Warif out. And never more so than now.

Before he replied, Warif tried to remember exactly what he'd told her and what he'd told Wagdi, both after he'd gotten out and earlier, during Wagdi's visits in those final months when they'd started to let people in to see him. Wagdi was the one who'd come. Despite his fears, his legendary timidity, he had come, which might have been why, no matter how frequent his visits, he aged so noticeably between one and the next. Or, at least, so it had seemed to Warif. Sally never visited him, but that hadn't upset him because she was with him in the cell much of the time, both after visits were permitted and before; if she was capable of hurting him or, to be precise, if he was capable of being hurt by her, then it would have been so much the worse for him. But she was like a goddess: the slightest gesture of affection—just having faith that she was out there, somewhere—was sufficient.

Sally herself had faith—had repeatedly made it clear in that confident-equivocal tone of hers—in a plurality of gods. In her view, it was the best way to reconcile the mysteries of life, the problem of evil, the random allotment of good fortune, the absurd cruelty of fate. He didn't like debating matters of faith with Sally. He was drawn, at least when he gave the matter any attention, to the idea that we were living in a simulation, and (again, when he could be bothered) could furnish a well-argued case that we existed within a construct created by the bored and none-too-competent programmers of another reality. The rapidly accelerating changes of recent times only strengthened his claim to this conceit, but Sally had little patience for the proofs he enumerated, and he wasn't interested in upsetting her. Whatever the reason for our existence, he was simply grateful that she was in his life. Watching her, he'd frequently find himself wondering: If man—in his fullest and most abstract sense, as it were—was beauty itself, then how should he see his corporeal self, how should he perceive the particularity of his body and its parts, how should he follow its movement through time and his surroundings? All of which he was quite incapable of explaining to her. These thoughts, when voiced, might unsettle the tranquility of that inner inquiry and make him cry, and so he simply said that he couldn't take in the sheer numbers of foreigners these days. That he'd had no idea there could be so many.

She shrugged, said, "Don't forget that tourism has been booming," then threw him a look. "You, of all people, shouldn't forget."

For sure, she had her moments, times she paid her dues to a cruel god. He thought back to the last time they'd met before he'd gone to prison. It was like she was living in a completely different country, one that knew nothing of the disturbances, striding through it all with head held high, a field wave untouched by other ripples or vibrations. She'd just terminated a third unwanted pregnancy, or was it the fourth? "Sent it back to heaven," she'd said. He'd pictured a great crowd of little creatures, all bearing her features in various combinations with those of other men, playing together in the sky and never growing old, every so often welcoming another brother or sister into the group. So many cradled between those slim hips, he thought: How many men had she met, befriended, and fucked—how many women? Thirty-two, she'd told him, not counting women. Then, with dignity, a finger held aloft: "But never two at once."

He didn't care to think about it. She gave herself to him now and then, and he had no desire to spoil things, or find things out about himself that he'd rather not know. Just her being there was all his life could handle, so he was content with that small part of her, which still filled him to the brim and overran. It was even true of those days of which he could remember only being asleep at her side; back in the apartment on Adly Street, into which he'd moved a few months before prison, its small window looking down on the dusty, silent synagogue.

Sally would come over frequently. The place was originally part of a larger apartment, which the building's owner had partitioned into two, creating a strange spatial distortion: a front room like a passageway, dwarfed by the cavernous bathroom and airy bedroom, then a living room ringed by doors. The place lived on in his imagination as a kind of amusement park. Sally used to walk in from the summer heat, already exhausted from her hunt for a Downtown parking space, and would head straight for the heart of the apartment, the living room that was sheltered from the heat of the exterior walls. When she slumped down beside him on the thick Persian rug, he would reach out to flick the switch on the ancient, floor-mounted air conditioner and together they'd doze off to its roar. They never talked much on such occasions; they'd sleep through the afternoon, wake to eat in silence, a cold whatever from the fridge, then sleep again: like narcoleptics, or as if the troubled world outside had ended and nothing was left to them but boredom, waiting. Like they'd returned together to a womb and were enveloped in its darkness, her drool wetting his neck, his nose snuffling her skin. Their dreams back then, he thought, had surely mixed together.

She'd wake as night fell, waking him. He might come around to find her body recovering itself from his, gently lifting his leg to extract her thigh, or cradling his head as she reclaimed her chest, or simply slipping out from between his arms. The moment of disentanglement made him feel dizzy, as though his blood pressure had dropped or he hadn't eaten for days: like he was abandoned, left alone to face his first day at school. Sometimes his eyes would snap open at the time she usually woke to find her still asleep, and it would feel as though they were so in harmony that her biological clock was driving his. On those occasions, he would keep quite still. Whether on top of her or under her, her around him or him around her, he would simply look at whatever the bluish light from the oddly proportioned entryway would permit: the green irises beneath her wide-shuttered lids, still visible by dint of imagination, by force of familiarity and fondness, and the blonde-brown streaked hair that was their shared pillow. Then her scent: milk and white wine. Till she woke, time didn't exist.

On that day, his hand gingerly crept out, hunting for his cigarettes, the sacred white Merits around whose continued availability all his budgeting revolved. In the blue dark, his fingers found the pack, but it was empty. As softly as possible he began to pull away from Sally, turning ghost as he undid himself. His back scraped the base of the old sofa at whose foot they'd been sleeping, and he noiselessly got to his feet, his darkness a silhouette against the window. Gently, gently, he shut the front door behind him, choosing not to call the elevator so that the *ting!* of its arrival wouldn't sound down the silent passage. Soft-footing it instead down seven flights of stairs.

He'd get a fresh pack from the little corner shop: across the street, past the permanent guard post outside the shuttered synagogue, then the wooden doorway of the discreet European restaurant. There was a light summer breeze blowing, finally finding its way through as the traffic and crowds thinned. Suddenly, he remembered that there was a second pack in the bag he'd left hanging in the entryway. He halted, almost turned back, then went on anyway. Why not another? He'd buy some of the German chocolates Sally liked.

Then a voice asked him the time. He stopped again, pulled out his phone, and looked at the clockface on his faintly glowing screen. A man with a thick mustache was moving to his side, and just as he was telling him the time, he noticed another man approaching from behind. Oddly, the street was empty. He saw the guards outside the synagogue slipping away into the night and heard the restaurant door click shut. Outside the corner shop, a diminutive man of about forty sat perched on an empty crate of spring water, his face turned away toward the taxis that jostled and fought for the few potential fares that still stood waiting at the intersection of Adly and Sharif. He felt the second man brush his back pocket and his whole body stiffened.

He thought of the disturbances that had finally died down a few days before. The first man was now asking him if he lived around here. He sounded like police. Warif nodded and pointed to the building where he lived, finger trembling despite himself. Later, he would feel ashamed for that, because Sally had been inside. But the two men didn't even look up. The second man slipped Warif's wallet from his back pocket with professional dexterity and took out the ID card, which he passed to his mustachioed colleague (who, Warif now saw, wore a service pistol on his hip) while he continued to pick through the wallet. With practiced ease his fingertips flipped through cards and receipts, then, with the abnormally long nail of his little finger, he eased open the little leather pockets, conducting his inspection despite the dimness of the light that filtered down from the few streetlamps left working by the power-saving measures still in force. By the same dim yellow wash, the mustachioed man was poring over the personal data printed on his ID. Warif prepared himself for questioning, but the man just pocketed the card:

"Give me your phone."

He gave him the phone. When he got it back, seven years later, he hadn't even recognized it.

He heard Sally ask, "Are your neighbors breeding curlews or something?"

Since getting out, he'd noticed massed choirs of birdsong, something he didn't remember from before. He replied that they (that's how he said it, without specifying which "they" they were) almost certainly had no interest in rearing anything of any beauty, and what's more, who ever heard of anyone breeding curlews, that most secretive of birds, anywhere, let alone here? Most likely, the song was coming from the newly planted palisade of bushes and trees across the street.

A few days ago, she said, she saw a little gazelle. It was in one of those extensions that the newcomers had added to al-Azhar Park; she'd spotted it as she wandered across the lawn, looking for somewhere to smoke away from prying eyes. There was this grassy little hillock, and she had just tucked herself behind it when she'd heard a soft, strange sound, like a sick foal, a thin whinny with a catch in it, and turning, she saw it, a tiny brown gazelle with ears like leaves. It was approaching her in starts, coming forward then shying, and all the while making this...this sound.

"It's called *salil*."

"What?"

"Salil," Warif said again. "A gazelle's call."

She stared at him, and he saw his shadow doubled in her green eyes. Whenever he came out with a word like that, it took him by surprise; the vocabulary built up inside during those long years as a translator—he just assumed that he'd lost it in prison, burned it up the way the body burns calories: mental fats and carbs that kept him going after all those failed attempts to drive himself insane.

The gazelle had reminded her of her mother, Sally added: the same green-gold eyes. He wanted to tell her she was wrong, that a gazelle's eyes can't be green, but didn't want to correct her twice in a row. When he first met her, she was always bringing up her parents. She'd been like a child, almost. How at parties she danced by bouncing up and down, or the way she still gave her age to the month: "I'm twenty-six and a half," she'd say, or, "I'll be twenty-eight in four months." Knowing what she did for a living, he found it hard to reconcile the gulf between its gravid tedium and the boisterous energy of her inner life. The world of women still lay behind locked doors, he thought.

Shortly after their first meeting, she told him that she knew him from Facebook. They were working together on some project run by the bank where she worked, an initiative to promote tourism. He was the go-between with the tourism ministry and the state information service, wandering into the job from the world of translation thanks to the influence of an uncle whom he'd met just once, on a toe-curling visit with his father. After graduating, he'd taken a position that straddled office and field, between the reptilian lethargy of a government office (chilled to near immobility by twentieth-century air-conditioning units whose ceaseless buzz filled the cavernous, humid libraries in the palaces of the grandees who'd built modern Egypt) and the pale winter sunlight whose wan allure was supposedly going to tempt waves of tourists and foreign delegations to the country. Sally, kind, green-eyed, with her deceptive childishness, belonged to a world of money, bank accounts, and budgets. Maybe, he thought, it was the bookkeeping that accounted for the months and weeks to which she calculated her age, not to mention (as he would discover shortly) her lists of lovers or the taxonomies of the gods in which she believed. After the foreigners started coming back, she reeled off numbers and types, increases and decreases as a percentage for each and every nationality. A vast database humming beneath that blonde-brown hair.

Once he was released, back to so-called freedom, she told him everything: it was his turn to sit and listen, to try and remember what it felt like to be surprised. In other words, the way she'd been with him when they first met: her gaze of admiration prompted by the way he wrote, the blend of wit and confidence and courage that she'd liked. Back then there had been a brief window when everyone could speak their minds, when the authorities were weak—licking their wounds perhaps, or laying plans for their next assault. Intellectually, he might not have been fully persuaded, but he allowed his innocent body to enjoy its freedom nonetheless: let it out of the cage, allowed his feet to go where they liked—down wrecked and unlit roads free of the state, into the itinerant markets that shifted from neighborhood to neighborhood, through the crowds that were emerging from their bolt holes and dark corners to fill the sunlit corniche, the open squares, the asphalt ribbons of the highways, with their joy and their hunger, eyes weak from the dark and the damp. He let himself taste new food, let his hips shake and sway at impromptu celebrations. He wanted happiness and he wanted death, and to him, back then, each seemed as romantic as the other. And finally, he allowed himself to think and to write, without counting the cost, without fear or revision. For the first and last time in his life he expressed what he felt. He wasn't scared of a knock on the door, of the figures in his dreams; the panic attacks were gone. He mocked himself, and the work his father had secured for him. He made fun of his father, himself, and the country, too, of history and destiny and "the people." But, also for the first time, he was without bitterness; his mockery was teasing, a rich man's playful ridiculing of the vagrant's life. And he and people like him were able to afford themselves this luxury because there were no consequences. His posts were shared everywhere, and Sally of course believed that this was him, that these words were his nature, that this intelligence and bravery was not an exception, but the essence of how he lived. When the bank's project brought them together, she waited till she was sure it was him, then confessed her admiration that, he quickly discovered, was not quite the simple admiration it had first seemed. After all, there was more to her than he had imagined.

She hadn't known her father long. He had lived and died in the quiet European city where she was born, had given her both a childhood worth remembering and a European passport, but it was her Egyptian mother who passed on those green eyes and would carry her back home to shelter in the lee of her Egyptian family, some of the last holdouts of the Heliopolis bourgeoise. She was a European, living a European life surrounded by Cairenes, but it amused her to irritate her family by asserting her Egyptianness, a version indebted to the black-and-white movies she adored. She ate at popular restaurants, frequented the markets in Bab al-Ghouriya, and wore the flapping robes popular with those cautious foreign women who followed the advice of guidebooks and consular advisories. But on the street they still shouted to her in English, and outside the business studies department her circle of acquaintances was limited to people she met at contemporary art exhibitions and the artists that frequented foreign cultural institutions. Her presence in these spaces, she thought, might be enough to balance out the data-processing and financial management that had staked their claim to her soul first during her years of study, then at her job at the investment bank, which the levelheaded European in her had accepted with exemplary pragmatism: the same clear-eyed attitude that spared her a more local sense of shame when it came to love. Her first lovers were from the art world, but she soon perceived the same old sexual complexes lurking just below a fragile veneer, and she grew more cautious and selective. Like everyone else during the years of political unrest she mixed with every type of person, and they all mixed with her. A world of worlds unfurled before her, behind every class and kind lay dozens more, and it was around this time, or shortly afterward, that she finally came face to face with Warif, as part of the bank's joint initiative with the tourist board. She remembered him almost immediately. At some point during the recent events, she'd followed him on Facebook.

There was something about the way he wrote: the blend of witty satire, the shimmer of his ideas, the well-concealed nihilism that underlay it all. She liked the way he looked in his photo, and she wasn't sure why. Did he remind her of someone? A former lover, maybe? Or did it go further back, to some long-buried memory of her northern childhood? A person can't always articulate what's going on inside them, and it wasn't as if she'd ever felt the need to get to know him in person, but when chance brought him into that other world, her world of work with its banks and commerce, its profits and budgets, she felt, obscurely, that a wish had been satisfied, that one of her gods had harbored a desire for her, of which she'd been ignorant. He had (this she remembered immediately after the meeting ended) stopped writing at exactly the same time as everyone else, and she might have forgotten him entirely; but when they came face to face, everything came back, and she almost cracked a smile as she suddenly remembered something he'd written, something that had kept her laughing for days. The truth was that, in person, he came across as considerably less worldly than his posts had made him seem, so much so that she took her time to be sure that it was him; indeed, she was only convinced by the long odds of that face and a name that unusual belonging to more than one person.

The night he didn't return she woke up in darkness and instantly sensed his absence. Sprawled out on the living-room carpet, surrounded by doors, she felt her body dropping into a vast void. The only sounds were the old air conditioner and the kitchen's neon hum. She remained as she was for several minutes then slowly clambered to her feet. Without him there it felt as though her body had shrugged off some gravitational force, but that same weightlessness ran a spasm down her back. She switched on the light and sat on the sofa, its gilt frame a reminder of former tastes. She suddenly realized that she'd never woken up there alone before. Needing to be sure, she went down the entryway's passage to the bathroom and for the first time was conscious of the peculiarity of the apartment's layout. She came back to the living room, got her cigarettes, then went to the kitchen and lit one off the burner. For a while she just stood there, not knowing what to do, not even knowing what she could do. She tried calling him from the living room, but he didn't answer. She stopped trying, put on her shoes, then tried again. The phone was off. She was scared now and told herself how stupid that was. She left the building and collected her car from the garage nearby. It was so dark out that for an instant she assumed there must have been a power outage. She left Downtown.

At home she checked Facebook. He'd posted nothing, didn't appear to have logged on recently. She looked at her phone. No calls from him and no messages.

A few days later, the rumor was confirmed, and she knew she wouldn't see him for a while, though she never expected it to last as long as it did.

3

WAGDI

Even in daylight, the giant screens along the main thoroughfare of the tiny island of Manyal were blinding. In Pasha Square they were crowded so thickly that they seemed more like a single vast surface constructed out of fragments of every shape and size, from the high-definition handheld devices of pedestrians to the looming holographic displays mounted on the buildings. Of these, Warif's attention was caught by one from which a kneeling redheaded woman seemed to be spilling onto the street. Dressed in a pink slip that rode up her thighs, her knees looked as though they might crush the neat rows of food trucks on the pavement below with their rotisserie spits, their couscous and tajines, pad Thai kung and som tam. No trace now of the old pickle carts, nor the shops where he used to buy jars of tirmes marinaded in paprika and other spices, nor the warm fragrances of biscuits made with baker's ammonia, black pans full of flaky, ghee-drenched fateer, or white rolls stuffed with pepper and cucumber and sold to schoolchildren. In their place were the glass fronts of chain cafés selling sandwiches and donuts, interspersed with outlets for fried rice and tacos, and on the corner, where he used to pick up the pungent fermented fish that was feseekh and ringa for his father, was American-style chicken. The true surprise was the survivor: the Faten Hamama cinema, still standing where the short bridge from the main corniche connected with the island, had been given a new lease on life. The three-arched facade had been reincarnated as something halfway between a tent and a pyramid; possibly a rose with its petals tightly closed, thought Warif as he stood there, stunned and squinting up at the Latin script of the cinema's name. Below the sign was an advertisement for the film currently being shown—Spanish, from the look of it—in which a thick-browed woman glared down at the broad street that cut through the city's gloom.

In his early 2000s Lanos, Wagdi had dropped Warif off at Downtown's new boundary line and driven on to his office in the south of city. Just like last time, he refused to walk with him through the heart of the newcomers' domain. His "Egyptian features," as he called them, brought him stares on the street, a hostile reception in restaurants, and occasionally harassment by security forces. These days, the security mostly comprised Eastern Europeans; it had become clear that the cost of the original batch of guards from the UK and Germany was unsustainable. Warif remembered the guard on the Corniche. Such vexations, and above all the attentions of the security guards, were a painful reminder to Wagdi of the pointlessness of the journalist pass he'd spent years working to obtain, only for the political unrest not only to render it useless, but to convert it into a target on his back. Then, with the arrival of the newcomers, it became an irrelevance; he was targeted for nothing more than the way he looked, which is to say Egyptian: the telltale signs of a poor diet, the ineradicable reek of his overactive adrenal gland that turned dogs' heads and made them bark as they singled him out amid the crowds.

His trouble with dogs had started long ago, as far back as his first forays beyond the bounds of his village. "I'm a coward from a village of cowards," he'd say, with an almost religious resignation. The dogs in the village were well accustomed to the haze of hormonal terror that hung about its inhabitants. It was only when they started attending secondary school in the nearby town that their problems began: bullied by everything from dogs to cats to rats, even the weasels that would brazenly curl around their ankles. For a good while Wagdi was half-convinced he must be invisible. He tried coaching his body and mind not to pump out the chemicals that drew them to him. The theory was that by confronting his fear with a dose of rational counterargument and calming common sense, the signals to his adrenal gland might, if only temporarily, be impeded, ensuring that he was only producing enough to keep himself in working order: that fear that is as necessary to us as the shock of pain. The technique had served him well enough to date, first through the years of normality, then the breaking storm and the madness that followed. His fear didn't just shield him from the major events, the random killing and detentions, but more importantly, from the dangers that came out of the blue without rhyme or reason: he learned to preempt them, avoiding potential classroom beatings and street robberies, rejections from girls who might otherwise have caught his eye. The wisdom of his cowardly forefathers taught him to hand things over before they were taken, to let it go before you could be rejected, to wash your unspoken opinions down with thick, bitter tea. But when Warif was jailed—one of the few people in whose presence he allowed himself to express his views before he could swallow them—the adrenaline returned, welling from every pore in his body until it made his heart turn somersaults just to open his mouth. The nightmares were overwhelming: waking visions at work, hearing his name called in the street, seeing people pointing angrily at him on public transport. He'd jump with fright when people brushed past him.

At the website's office they suggested he take time off, but the thought of being alone in the matchbox he rented in Boulaq al-Dukrur was too much; panic-stricken, he began hunting for anything, anyone, to take his mind off it all and finally he found what he was after with a colleague. Souad. A low-level administrator, she had been promoted to manage social media sites, a move that fulfilled both her career ambitions and an innate fondness for cost-cutting measures. Neither a city girl nor a villager, she came from one of those peripheral, semirural limbos. For her, then, their post-marriage move to Ard al-Liwa hardly felt like a step up in life, though it did spare her the hour-and-a-half bus journey to work. Then she had Ahmed and Zeinab, both of whom took after her, and when everything changed they moved again, into one of the tall, skinny tower blocks beyond the ring road. Work was farther away, sure, but the new buildings and shimmering asphalt, the clean smell of the desert nearby, was to her infinitely preferable, classier than the shattered, half-dirt roads with trash heaps smoldering on the corners, thugs battling it out in broad daylight, and a fog of hash smoke by night. Then, with no warning, the website shut down. Souad stayed at home while Wagdi was promoted to a better position, more aligned with the recent developments. For the first time since she'd known him, he seemed enthusiastic; he mentioned the possibility of moving to a bigger apartment. Then the fear returned. Of course, she'd never seen him that way, and tried to extract some kind of explanation, but Wagdi, a veteran of glandular regulation, managed to bring things back under control.

When he heard that prison visits had recently been approved again, Warif returned to him with redoubled force. Almost every night, their old friendship would figure in his dreams—curbside chats, card games in the cafés, long confessionals in Downtown bars—and the odd thing was that, in his sleep at least, it was he who was angry with Warif, not the other way round. The source of that anger being that his excuses had run out. He would not be able to turn his back on what was happening; he must overcome the chemicals pumping through his body, his inherited fear, and visit him in prison.

Three days in a row he attended the wake for Warif's parents, not even knowing whether his friend had the faintest idea of his loss. In the years leading to that moment, he'd imagined Warif sitting with his knees pulled to his chest in some shadowed and forgotten pit, a deep well in an unpeopled forest. By the time he went to see him, sitting on one side of an almost invisible glass panel with a two-way speaker in front of him, everything had changed for good and he realized he'd really known nothing. Warif was aware of what was going on outside, albeit the image he received was both hazy and behind the times. By the time he got out a few months later, the moment of release had lost its filmic grandeur. Before, prisoners would file out like ants as the two huge gates swung open to the empty desert and a single ribbon of asphalt that would carry them back to life, the past left behind them like a dream. No more. Now, he left through a door that could have been the entrance to a company headquarters or an institute, to a mall even, to be conveyed in Wagdi's Lanos back to his parents' dust-dressed apartment. The apartment was on Adly Street, so the drive took a while. On one of his previous, rare forays to Downtown, Wagdi had noticed a group of what he took to be Russians leaving the building, and couldn't shake the idea that they were living in his friend's place.

Today, though, he dropped him at the ring-road's off-ramp, on the outskirts of Old Cairo, and drove on to the job he'd managed to retain despite everything.

Warif kept walking north till he came to the little bridge that linked the island with the al-Malik al-Saleh. Music blared and graffiti artists were everywhere; beneath the bridge he could see ducks and geese drifting along peacefully, here and there spun by small eddies. The silent fishermen who once ranged along the banks by the Qasr al-Einy hospital, or dropped their lines over the gunwales of the old river boats, were gone, and with time on his hands he slowed, strolling spellbound past the dancing screens, knocked and bumped by passersby of every nationality. He was pondering Sally's comment about tourism and the sarcasm of his response, when he realized with a start that he was already late for his appointment. Quickening his pace, he wound his way to Manasterly Palace, assuming the department he wanted would be located inside, but once there his phone instructed him to keep going, then take a right, up to a set of gates that were almost hidden by a stand of still trees. A villa with its own little garden. There was no one there, so he went in, and as he did so a bright patch of something floated down from a tree onto the lawn. A hoopoe. Its thin beak tugged something from the soil and then Warif had the impression that it looked at him, a quick glance from the corner of its eye before it flapped back up to its hidden perch among the flowering branches. At the entrance he did as they'd requested in a message sent to him the day before, touching his phone to a little screen beside the door. A green light blinked, there was a click, and the door opened. Warif pushed it wider and went in.

There was nobody inside either. Facing him, just as in a scene from some black-and-white movie, a broad central staircase split into two thinner flights, one curving to the right, the other to the left. Quite alone, as though returning home, he crossed the atrium and began to climb. In the absence of any other sound, he could hear the squeak of his soles against the marble. He took the lefthand flight up to the second floor, and once on the landing found an arrow on the wall pointing upward and beside that a second staircase, this one wooden and much narrower. He climbed again. These stairs were noisier, and when he got to the top he heard the sound of other people for the first time, the soft murmur of voices speaking in multiple languages. And there was another arrow, this one pointing to an office on his right. The door was as white as the wall, as though camouflaging itself, and there was no handle, so he knocked softly. A voice, in English, asked him to come in.

The office was very small indeed, at least compared to the one in which he'd met the unplaceable man, but shared the same powerful and seemingly unsourced glare. This time, there was a woman behind the desk. She was in her late fifties, perhaps, kind-looking and casually dressed; she might have been sitting on her balcony at home. She welcomed him and asked him to sit on the only other chair. Her accent was more obvious, though: definitely Eastern Europe, Slavic. His instincts, or say, his professional experience, were telling him she was Czech. When he sat down and faced her he noticed that despite her amiable air, her eyes were hard.

The smell of coffee rose from the brown mug in her hand as she peered at a screen that, even to Warif, fresh from prison, looked outdated. The woman kept removing then replacing her glasses, as though unused to them, but her eyes never left the screen. Then she smiled. "It seems someone's made a mistake. Your request has been sent to me without your personal information..."

Not knowing what to say, Warif just raised his eyebrows. Was the office a touch chilly, he wondered? Maybe cold was how she liked it. She continued, "Don't worry though, the file should be along any second. And here it is..."

From where he sat, he watched her move the mouse and start to read, and despite himself, he tried to picture it, the file that contained his life. How much would it weigh on paper? Had they had to compress the data? But perhaps they'd sent her an edited version, because only seconds later, the woman was looking up and speaking to him, this time to make the very point that Sally had made.

"No," he said. "I haven't received my first salary payment, and I don't want it. That's if you could call it a salary. I never worked for it."

"That's how it is for all citizens," she said quickly. "If salary doesn't work for you, let's call it a stipend. Or a pension, say. I think they have an official term for it now, anyway, something like an 'associate card.'"

"Look, my issue's not with the name of the thing..." he began, but she cut him off with a quick nod, "Yes, you want to return to your former position. The truth is we hardly ever have to deal with that particular request. Personally speaking, I'd love to get paid for doing nothing. If you didn't..."

It was his turn to interrupt.

"You mean, if I didn't know certain people then I wouldn't have been able to get this appointment? Her name's Sally, by the way."

A smile.

"No need to upset yourself. Would you like something to drink?"

He shook his head impatiently then realized that she was waiting for him to speak. He wanted to lay everything out as clearly as possible, but for some reason he found that the words wouldn't come. The silence stretched out for a few moments more, then she said, "You know, I've heard a few things. Is it true that you have something to do with…"—she waved her free hand vaguely—"all that?"

Warif thought for a second. "I don't know. Might be. But maybe it was just a coincidence."

She was watching him intently.

"Sometimes," he went on, slowly, "the thought that it could be true does frighten me. On the other hand, the idea that it isn't feels like an absurd joke."

A smile spread across her face.

"Whatever the case, there's no need for that frown of yours. You might not believe it, but there's a good chance that your request will be granted."

This was a surprise. He'd weighed the odds as somewhere between difficult and impossible and now he felt an almost overpowering urge to confront her with the dozens of questions that had been crowding his mind. With a great effort he restrained himself; once the floodgates of inquiry were opened, they would be difficult to close. Something in his expression made her chuckle, and she turned back to the screen briefly to make an entry.

"Done. I've sent your file on. There's just a few hoops left to jump through and you should be back in your old job in no time."

As he rose to his feet and left the room, he felt weightless. Walking to the gate, he again had the sensation that he was home. He looked around for the hoopoe but saw only lawn and trees. He heard music from the street outside, a song that reminded him of children's parties, and walking out, he followed the sound until he saw an ice-cream truck. It was strange to see it here, with winter just around the corner. Behind the truck's sliding glass window was a young woman wearing a sort of beret and a black-and-pink uniform. He glanced around, half-expecting to see children running out from buildings and side streets, and now he really did wish he lived here. The first two children appeared, trotting excitedly toward the truck. He watched their approach with affection, trying to work out where they were from. Overhead, a breeze moved the branches. A light rustling started up. He imagined the hoopoe hidden by the canopy, holding fast to its perch, then remembered that hoopoes build their nests in the trunks of trees, out of the wind. Now more children were coming, surging toward the truck, and it was then that it hit him.

Thirty-two years full of reasons to be afraid, followed by seven in prison—six and a half of them spent in a state not unlike death itself. Here, on the pavement beneath the trees, a few yards from Manasterly Palace, facing the cheerful spectacle of children clustered around an ice-cream truck, just as he was beginning to sense the faint stirrings of a hope he hadn't known for years, Warif had a panic attack.

Like he had no feet. Like he was floating, not in the air, but inside himself. It was a raw terror of a kind he'd never experienced, not when the heavy boots were slamming into his head and ribs and he was convinced he was going to die, nor when he sat detained in that historical building in Talaat Harb while life went by on the street outside and the sounds of television and laughter filtered down from the floors above, nor even through those nightmarish hallucinations and dreams in his cell: his father squatting in the corner in his burial shroud, searching for his mother's grave among the holes and cracks of the crumbling wall or scrabbling in the street for his eyeball dislodged by a punch. Never anything like this fear, which seeped in through every pore. This icy cold, this sense of falling into himself like he was a well, like he was a stone falling down that well. Unable to stand, he lowered himself to the curb, wishing that he was back in the apartment, but though he managed to sit, his head still felt as if it were floating. He could see the children around the truck, and he told himself that this was it, here was death at last, it was over. This is how he was going to go, surrounded by strangers, stretched out on the pavement like a dog.

4

THE FUTURE

Sally hadn't lied to him, nor had she been imagining things. He could see them himself, hopping here and there behind the green banks. And not only gazelle: there was a big buck hare, sitting up on its hind legs and staring straight at him. At least that's what it looked like, sitting at a distance with its brown eyes fixed on him. Did all the animals here watch the visitors?

Having asked himself the question, he reconsidered. Visitors wasn't quite the word. The park stretched away seemingly without end. There were no walls that he could see, and the people scattered everywhere, singly and in groups, seemed perfectly relaxed, scarcely conscious of the world outside—in fact, it was as though they were at home. He saw stands of beech and cherry and cypress, streams running between oaks and redwoods, and then he saw himself, some day in the future, a sleeping bag beneath his arm as he pushed deeper and deeper into a darkness that thickened around the trunks of hornbeam and lemon, and never coming back.

He thought about how the grass he lay on now was itself laid over the dividing line between the neighborhood around Salah Salem Street and the district made up of the Ghaffir cemetery and Mansheyat Nasr's tangle of roads. He'd been coming here for several days straight, taking advantage of his white-passing skin and the appointment passcodes still stored on his phone, but nobody so much as looked his way, let alone challenged him. After collapsing in the street he'd been in a state of constant terror, but then, surfacing in his memory like a point of light, came the conversation with Sally about the little gazelle and the parklands, so here he was, stretched out on the grass until he was almost lost in it, a flower.

After the first panic attack there had been others, but less powerful, like an earthquake's aftershocks. He had read up on them and what he read helped a little and confused him a lot, but he did manage to establish that panic attacks tend to strike the unhappy if they smile without warning, like a backwash of bad luck, that they have arms to reel you back in if you try to flee, that they always remind you when you start to forget. At home, he wanted to get out; out on the street he wanted to go home to hide and be alone with his distress. If he took refuge in crowds, it held him apart from them, mocking his desperation: bleeding out sweat and surrounded by their indifference, dropping down the well as he stood still, their voices fading. He'd want to weep, and when he couldn't, would just take off, striding away with no clear destination, his eyes wide. It was in flight from just such an attack that his feet brought him to the square in Roda where the old al-Einy Palace had stood. The winter sun bleached the wooden walkways and stone stairs that crisscrossed the square and gleamed off the varnished tabletops and food trucks. Tourists and residents strolled or sat on the benches. Warif had lowered himself onto the curb that faced a hill-like rise to one side of the square and was watching people come and go, eyes swimming from the glare and the tears that still clung there, when from a group of young people passing by came a shout:

"Come on man... Smile!"

He froze for a moment, but they were cheerful enough, and he did his best to return their grins. He felt old.

But he also felt hungry, so he got to his feet and went up to one of the food trucks that, to his surprise, was selling beer with the food. He approached the counter, but the woman inside rather sternly instructed him to join the queue. She muttered something in a language he couldn't quite catch, and several customers turned to stare. The queue ran sideways along the paneling of the truck, not perpendicular to the counter, as he would have expected. He shambled to the end of the line, waited, and when he at last made his order he handed the woman a few extra coins, but she neither smiled nor thanked him. Beer and corndog in hand, he went back to the square, this time to one of the wooden tables. As he sipped the beer, he thought he could smell the Nile nearby. He finished the dog, impaled on its plastic stick, and a sparrow landed on the table, hopped closer, and stood there calmly. It shifted closer still and stared at him. Warif found himself smiling back. He remembered another sparrow that had stared at him. It used to watch him from a hole high up in the wall of his cell. His heart clenched in his chest and he left.

When Wagdi, without much hope of success, invited him to dinner at his place the next day he was astonished to find the invitation accepted. Warif couldn't have said why he'd agreed, whether he was looking for an escape from his fear or simply that his willpower was drained, but he gave in almost without thinking, without the energy to stave off his

SLEEP PHASE

friend's insistence. Later, he'd wonder whether some small spark of curiosity hadn't played a part in his decision, a desire to pry into a world he'd left long ago and to which he was scared to return, a world that had shuttered and bolted its windows behind him. A visit to Wagdi's was an adventure of sorts, then, and the price was negligible. A free ticket to a horror movie.

Nothing was different. The majority of the buildings might have been brand new, but otherwise the neighborhood was a carbon copy of their old one, resurrected in the desert beyond the ring road: high tower blocks facing each other, lines of garbage along the curb as though kicked aside by giant feet as they passed. There were peels and stalks from the grocers' carts clogging the gutter, opposing rows of gridlocked cars, their bumpers meshing, café chairs strewn randomly over the sidewalks, shisha smoke weaving into proteinous clouds over the cheap restaurants before which cats skulked in hopes of free pickings while dogs lounged, resting before their night shift beneath the neon that shivered above the doors of the little shops and the yellow glow of the kiosks' lightbulbs, children playing in the street, shouting and sprinting between the cars. Then there was the smell that floated through the window of Wagdi's car to assault Warif's nostrils: like a blend of it all, even the light and noise. The window: looking out now he saw only women, and only a few of them, striding purposefully and never turning, either carrying black bags or, the younger ones at least, talking into their phones. From speakers on all sides, the call to evening prayer began to sound as Wagdi pulled over, and they both unfolded into the stew of noise and odors. They were carried up by a cramped little elevator whose mirror, cracked in the top-right corner, contrived to make the atmosphere more depressing still.

He had the strangest sensation that he'd never met Souad before. From the moment he walked in and sat down till the moment he left, it was like he had no memory of her, even though he knew he'd met her on those occasions he'd visited Wagdi at work. This took him back to his second year in prison, when his memories of people began to lose their faces, their heads blank as pawns. With the exception of Sally, of course, whose opinion on the matter he would solicit as she pulled her legs tight to her chest to make room for them both in his solitary cell. He drove these thoughts from his mind and bent to hug the children and give them sweets. They looked just like Souad, as if she were their only parent, and were staring at him with a kind of wonderment. He realized that Wagdi didn't have many people round. It would be the younger of the two, Zeinab, who'd later be the first to notice the symptoms of his sickness, but right now, that is to say ten minutes after they'd walked through the door, Souad had finished laying out supper and was calling them all to the table.

That his stomach would be incapable of handling such a feast was not something that had occurred to him. Confronted with homemade messaqah with minced meat, fingers of stuffed cabbage, slices of roasted duck with orange, and a molokhiyya stew prepared with all Souad's experience and love, his guts rebelled. Swallowing the third mouthful, it struck him that it had been seven years since a meal like this—the food he'd been raised on—had passed his lips. He thought of his mother in the kitchen, working the suggestions of his Syrian aunts into Egyptian dishes. But he'd come home from prison to her absence. Ever since, he'd been eating canned food and takeout, and as he sat there, picking at the meal that Souad and Wagdi had served him in a neighborhood both brand new and the very pattern of the old, he saw that he had forgotten the concept of food altogether. For a few moments, he simply sat there, gaping at the laden table, aware of, but indifferent to, their stares. He saw Souad smile as she heaped more onto his plate, and as she did he remembered that tooth in her lower jaw, slightly set back from the rest of the row, the tooth that had always held a strange attraction for him, and suddenly he felt himself sweating, pouring sweat. Then his guts turned against him. It started with growls from his belly, growing louder and louder until he blushed. He stopped eating and took a gulp of water, only to feel the food rising back up his throat. He shut his mouth and clapped a hand over it. Now his hosts could tell that something was wrong. Did he want the bathroom, perhaps?

His head was lowered over the bowl but nothing would come up. Clambering to his feet, he took down his pants, turned, and sat, but still nothing, just the growls from his stomach. When at last he felt the sweats had passed, he stood again, hitched up his pants, and went to the sink. His face in the mirror looked pale. Out of the blue, he remembered that he still hadn't visited his parents' grave. Their portrait, hanging on the wall of his apartment, had lulled him into the false impression that their incessant bickering and sniping was, somewhere and somehow, going on unabated. He had no idea how long he stared into the bathroom mirror before he heard Wagdi's tentative knock at the door. Was he all right?

Souad forced a smile but couldn't hide her irritation. "Did we manage to poison you, Warif?"

"He's gotten used to Swiss food," Wagdi said hastily, before Warif could reply.

The reference to prison flustered Souad. She

brought their tea out to the balcony and retreated inside, marveling at their desire to sit outside in such cold weather. It was cold, but the friends were reviving an old habit, dating back to the days of cheap student housing in the narrow streets around Giza. From the eleventh floor, the street was a little string, the traffic a rumor. Once again, he had the impression that Wagdi was aging at an incredible pace. He looked like one of those world-worn uncles you'd come across at every funeral back in the old days. I suppose I must too, he told himself, though it hadn't shown in the mirror. As he thought this, he had another thought: that neither of them had yet turned forty. Anyway, his stomach was quieter now. The heavy tea, coupled with the familiar buzz from the street and the patterned sounds of the power outage—the noise of children shouting from apartment windows around them instantly dampening as it came back on—made him feel, however briefly, that the years gone by were just an illusion, that the last three-quarters of his life had never taken place at all, and that all this—Wagdi with Warif, tea on the balcony, Souad with the kids inside—was a vision in a dream from his childhood. That he was, right then, just a boy, dozing fitfully after a heavy meal in the family apartment in Famm al-Khaleej.

For all Wagdi's unaccustomed confidence in Warif's company, his temporary sense of being liberated from his usual reticence, it was silence—that true proof of friendship—that dominated the time they spent together. Whether squeezed together on the balcony that Wagdi had shared with other students in Faisal, stretched out on the untended lawns at the Faculty of Literatures, or hunched over the little tables of Bar Hawaii in Fouad Street, the ritual was always the same: sipping tea in silence. Like in one of those jokes about Tibetan monks, one of them could make a comment and hours would pass before the other replied. They had an unspoken agreement about the basic principles of life, for the most part never put to the test, and over the years it had only deepened and grown richer. Even during that first prison visit Wagdi might not have asked him anything at all, had convention not required a "How are you?" Then the silence had descended again, and Warif had found it difficult enough to voice a simple, "Fine."

Right at the end, when permission for visits was given, the prison was still recovering from the effects of the sandstorm and the emergency repairs that followed. From the brink of death and oblivion, barely two weeks after he had been in his cell, struggling to keep his nose above the rising sands, Warif found himself thrown back in contact with the world. Even before the storm, he'd assumed that nothing remained of the world outside. Over the last couple of years he'd been overcome by a strange kind of calm, first surrendering to the routine then *becoming* it, to the extent that he sometimes wondered if, were the cell door to swing open and he be asked to leave, he might feel the same irritation we experience when dragged from the house to attend an unexpected but compulsory social event, or are forced to go hunting for a handyman.

As Warif lay on the dewy lawn of the endless park, floating over the ghosts of the tombs they'd dug up and deposited at the desert's fringe, he thought back to what Wagdi had told him as they'd finished the first cup of tea and how, unable to contain himself and for the first time in forever, he had smiled. Wagdi now worked in the channel's "future news" department and had just been preparing a report. In this new era of stability, with everyone receiving a regular salary and it being in all their interests to maintain the status quo, entertainment was the most important commodity of all: whatever it took to keep audiences (local audiences that was; the newcomers had their own interests, channels, and languages) glued to their many and various screens. In this new era, when nothing happened—nothing that concerned the locals at any rate, who were quite content with a set of circumstances more comfortable than any they'd known before—there was no need to cover breaking news. In fact, given that the news consisted of entirely fictionalized events, it could be prepared in advance, the ground laid for what would happen later, or for what they would give the impression was happening, when eventually the due date for its hypothetical happening rolled around.

Wagdi had been told to draw up a schedule for the next four weeks' worth of news, from mid-October to mid-November. Thinking of things to happen wasn't the problem. After two decades as a reporter, he was well versed in what went into a compelling story and the ingredients of a successful trend. No: Wagdi's efforts, his "struggle" as he sometimes liked to call it, revolved around two central questions. One: Should a news report describe an event that had really taken place, or was it only that the audience must believe that it had? For instance, if a famous and widely beloved actress was reported as having divorced her B-list singer husband, did their separation have to be supported by documentation? What would it mean to claim she'd made a sudden, shocking return to the arms of her former spouse? A union before a notary public and witnesses, a new marriage contract, and all the rest of it? Or was it only important that the audience be convinced that the events were true: the bickering and trial separation, the midnight quarrels and running fights in the streets, all placed on record by online rumors and leaked calls, anonymous witness statements, blurry photos snapped from car windows, silent CCTV footage of hotel corridors…?

"Which leads me to the second point…"

Wagdi had prepared a second round of tea, and now, with the chatter from the children's bedroom finally silenced, he continued. So, in the space between actual events and their portrayal, there is a margin for play in which the protagonists of said events might fall prey to violence or illness, might be confined to a hospital bed or see their careers destroyed; a space in which the boundary between reality and PR is blurred. If your job is just to make up these events—working (it goes without saying!) in collaboration with the protagonists—then not only do you avoid the possibility of material harm coming to them—something Wagdi regarded as a priority—but it also allows you to write up news much further in advance. Instead of a four-week lead or even a couple of months, the media can create a news schedule for the coming year, and can do so without inconveniencing the story's main characters. Is there anything finer than laying plans in advance, saving all your energy for the refinement and fine-tuning that turns your story into the truth itself? A truth, moreover, that is a genuine consolation for an audience that is persecuted by the existential questions that swarm into the vacuum in which they find themselves—these idle days with which they've been blessed?

Despairing of lazy colleagues who never exerted themselves beyond the absolute minimum, Wagdi had thought that Warif might help him draw up the schedule, to come up with suggestions and improvements.

"Wouldn't you like to write a story?" he asked with a smile. "Tell me what's going to happen tomorrow or next week?"

The idea was attractive enough. In some sense he'd be creating something; it would be like having a magic power to shape the future. But all the same, Warif wasn't convinced that Wagdi really needed his help. Plus, he still needed time to understand what was going on, let alone involve himself in shaping it. He had to absorb the present before he could start making the future. Maybe Wagdi just wanted someone to talk to, or maybe he was trying to distract Warif from his disorientation and the panic attacks. Perhaps it was his way of drawing Warif out, encouraging him to talk about his efforts to recover a semblance of his former life—or even about Sally, who had once again been out of contact, ever since the night she told him about the gazelle and they talked about the birds. But Warif knew she might reappear just as unexpectedly; he could sense her presence during his appointments. Answering his interviewers, he spoke as though she were watching, making sure he was on his best behavior—nothing like the way she'd been in his cell, when all she'd wanted was for him to tell her everything, about the madness most of all.

But someone was talking to him. He opened his eyes. A girl with braided brown hair was leaning over him, a tall young man behind her. The girl's eyes were narrowed, as though she were peering at the sun, and she was asking him if he was all right.

"Just fine," he said. "I must have dozed off."

A little confused and self-conscious, he got to his feet and gave them both an awkward smile. "Thanks."

He found himself wandering farther into the endless green. In a stand of elms and tulip trees, he was surprised to see the flowers on the tulips still glowed a fierce red in defiance of autumn's onset. Once desert, the turf beneath his feet was thick and springy, while the trees' canopies were like pyramids whose broad bases had collapsed or melted into one another. On the far side of the stand was another expanse of lawn, and just as he was asking himself if the time had maybe come to leave, he noticed objects moving in the sky overhead. He stopped and looked up. They were yellow and red and moving fast, falling at a steep angle toward the skyline, and then he noticed that they were throwing out something as they fell, two small things in pairs. He narrowed his eyes and realized that he was looking at parachutes: a cloud of brightly colored parachutes making for a patch of flat ground covered in white markings. He watched as one of the parachutes came to earth, the person beneath it touching down and sprinting furiously toward the green line of the horizon.

5

GHOSTS AT THE DOOR

Their accents, or at least that of the man who'd spoken, were Scandinavian, but the thing that really stood out was their extraordinary physiques, identical and somehow far too large for the size of the office. One entire wall was a window—this time the strength of the light made sense.

Both men were very tall, and it felt as though the only way they could be in here at all was if someone or something had built the tiny room around them. Facing the glass wall there was a single desk, which seemed logical enough; the room wasn't big enough for one of them, let alone both, and they surely didn't work here. In other words, they were here for him.

Neither sat at the desk, but rather side by side in two chairs, both angled toward Warif, who sat midway between them with his back to the door and his face to the window's glare. He had the sudden thought that they resembled a kind of insect he'd once seen long ago, but he couldn't remember whether it had been in a documentary or out in a field. It was the green shirt and pistachio-colored trousers of the man to his right that had prompted the thought; now he asked himself if he had ever seen anyone dressed like that outside of the army.

The man to his left, in a shirt so utterly unremarkable that it seemed to have no color at all, now turned to Warif, swinging his bony knees around like the muzzle of a double-barreled shotgun being brought to bear.

"But have you received your salary yet, Mr. Warif?"

Straight to the point, then. Warif had no desire no relitigate definitions of salary versus stipend. He had received no payments at all, he explained to the man, because he had never completed the procedure for obtaining one.

"Receiving a payment would mean prejudicing the outcome of my request."

The man in the green shirt said, "But at least you have an idea of the sum you'd be owed?"

"A very generous sum, yes. A lot of money. But that's not the issue."

"You want to return to your former job?"

"Well, it's the only job I have, isn't it?"

"Because that's where you were employed when you went to prison, correct?"

"Right."

"And your conviction had nothing to do with your work?"

Warif didn't know what to say. The answer was both yes and no, but he wasn't sure if the men were capable of understanding this. Then both of the men were speaking, taking turns:

"We're aware that things were somewhat different then."

"It's just that, even so, the reason for your sentence isn't exactly clear."

"You weren't particularly active. In politics, I mean. Revolutionary stuff, delinquency."

"However, there seems to be a suggestion, no more than a rumor, I'm sure, that you had something to do with what happened."

"If that's the case, then in my view you deserve to be compensated."

"The problem is that your request to be reinstated isn't straightforward."

"Not just because it would go against the current regulations."

"Forgive me for saying so, but you're also no longer the best-qualified candidate for the position."

"We're aware, of course, that your former

profession really has no relevance in a local context."

"I mean, you're a translator."

"If you were to accept the salary, or stipend if you prefer, that would, in our view, be the best solution. Just like every other local citizen."

"Frankly, we envy your position."

"I mean, I wish I could swap my job for sitting back and doing nothing!"

Warif was turning his head from left to right, back and forth between them. They looked like robots. The light from the window was so strong it hurt his eyes. Thinking back to what the woman had told him in the office by Manasterly Palace he wondered now why she'd seemed so optimistic, but the conviction he'd heard in her voice gave him the courage to respond, "I appreciate your perspective, gentlemen, but I'm asking myself if this is your opinion or a final decision?"

They exchanged a look. Even their faces are thin, thought Warif. The man in green said, "It's our opinion that you should hear our opinion."

The other said, "Whether or not you pursue this application is entirely your decision."

"There'll have to be a psychological evaluation, of course."

"Years in prison can take a toll."

"And we'll have to clear a few things up."

"Sort rumors from facts."

"Nevertheless…we remain hopeful."

"We'll find a way to resolve this, though we might not know how just yet."

"You might change your mind in the end."

"But you won't be our problem then."

Warif felt a faint dizziness coming on as he left the building, its broad front facing what had formerly been the ragged Dar al-Uloum Park on the fringes of Sayyida Zeinab, but was now a large egg-shaped building in and out of whose entrance strode young men and women in workout gear, their backs straight and heads held high. The third or perhaps fourth time that they'd met, Sally had stopped him in the street. She'd maneuvered behind him and placed her hand on his shoulder, then with a palm on his lower spine, had forced his back straight. The moon had been full over the Aboul Feda Corniche, and he'd felt her breasts against his back. The touch alone, a sensation he'd spent the following night sleeplessly contemplating, had more than made up for the wound that she'd opened, the memory of his father constantly criticizing him for hunching then giving up on him in despair. The intrusion of his father had been faintly distressing, but also unclear: Had he really thought of his father that night, after coming home from his walk along the Corniche with Sally, or was it only now that he was thinking of him, on the street that still had the name of Mubtadiyan? It frequently happened that, when he woke, he'd feel he had dreamed the same dream before, though he was never able to be sure. During the years in prison, after what he'd tried to do to his mind there, his thoughts had started to tangle, or to careen off one another like billiard balls.

The pedestrians moved in flocks, most of them coming from Qasr al-Einy Street. It was clear that the majority were tourists. They had that look: the wide grins, the unguardedly curious glances, the cameras hanging from their necks. One of the officers had asked him about tourists the night they'd detained him as he went to buy cigarettes and a bar of chocolate for Sally. It was in the basement of that building in Talaat Harb Street, after they'd dragged him away beneath the weak lamplight down Adly Street, across the intersection with Sharif, and into the darkness where Adly met Talaat Harb. To their right, Omar Effendi had been closing for the night; the lights of the department store were already off, and he remembered a woman in a black hijab passing them on the sidewalk and throwing a quick glance his way as she'd gone by. She had been, he thought now, the last woman he'd see for seven years; that is, if he didn't count Sally's visits to his cell, just as unpredictable and fleeting as they were outside.

As he'd gone with the two men, he'd told

himself that it was here at last, the thing he'd heard and read so much about, happening to him. His left knee had been trembling violently, he remembered, and perhaps his teeth had been chattering, too. He'd tried to soothe himself with the thought of the precautions he'd taken. By that point, having realized that deleting the app altogether would have looked suspicious, he'd been using a fake Facebook account. His regular account had his real name and face, friends who didn't move in troublesome circles, and the posts were all links to songs or movie clips, mixed with frequent and fervent statements in support of the al-Ahly football club. He made sure to update it regularly, and followed a few sports and music pages, too, even a couple of scholarly ones: a convincing simulacrum, at least to the casual glance, of a perfectly unremarkable life—indistinguishable from that of the thousands, if not millions, of other citizens who were completely uninterested in anything outside of football, tunes, and jokes about the differences between men and women. His alarm at the two men asking him to accompany them after a quick search through his phone was therefore balanced by a certainty that the account he was signed into was the clean one. The accounts shared a few names, though; or maybe they'd realize his ID had been used to make both.

At one old building they stopped and went in through the Italianate wrought ironwork of its entrance. It was dark inside, and there was a disagreeable smell like damp carpet. One of the men ordered him to sit. His trembling left knee bumped someone else's, and he hopped back then lowered himself to the ground cautiously, careful not to touch anything else. As his eyes grew accustomed to the gloom, he saw the entrance open and close again, and it was then that he realized the hall was packed with people, lots of them, and that most if not all were young men. He tried to work out if they had anything in common, but the light was too dim and his mind too preoccupied to reach any conclusions. He was thinking of Sally, at that very moment asleep on the carpet in that living room ringed by doors. How insignificant the distance between them right now. A few dozen meters? A hundred at most. But as things stood, those few meters were immeasurably vast. He wondered if she'd woken up yet. Was she surprised not to find him lying next to her, waiting for her to open her eyes? Would she call? Which brought him back to his phone, which was still with the men.

It hurt to sit cross-legged and hunched, and he leaned back, trying to find the wall, but the first thing his back met was some kind of metal pipe. For water, perhaps, or gas. Despite its unpleasant chill, he rested against it to give his knees a break. From somewhere came a buzzing; a little while later, he realized it was a television playing on some darkened floor above them. From time to time, he could make out, or thought he could make out, soft laughter.

The entrance opened again, and a name was called. At the far end of the hall, a shadow stood upright and tentatively went over. A young man, carrying what could have been an old Samsonite suitcase. A door-to-door salesman, Warif thought. The men who'd stopped him now entered and, while one watched silently, the other conducted an interrogation in a soft whisper. Neither his questions nor the young man's panicked answers were audible, despite the hush that lay over the huddle of men in the darkened hall. It struck Warif that the unpleasant smell was the smell of fear. Then, to his surprise, he saw the men hand back the young man's phone and ID and let him leave. The same ritual was repeated several times—a murmured interrogation, a young man exiting through the wrought iron entrance—and it started to feel as though the crowd in the hall was thinning out, that spaces were opening up. The first stirrings of hope swept over them. Warif began to think that he might even catch Sally before she left, maybe before she woke. But this was only because his sense of time had become unmoored in the darkness, the distinction between hours and dragging minutes impossible to make. It proved optimistic. The questioning stopped for a while, then resumed, and when the hall was almost empty, when it was just him and two or three others—plus the horde of insects that he could sense moving, half wondering whether he was imagining them—he finally heard a bored voice call his name.

The voice was so drab, so everyday that he almost didn't react. It was only when he got to his feet and felt his muscles cramp, and at the same time realized there were almost no people or cars moving past the entrance outside, that he knew how long he must have been sitting there. Beside the two who'd brought him in, there was now a third man, taller and slimmer than both and seemingly younger. In a confident, assertive tone, he asked Warif where he lived. When Warif told him, he seemed unpersuaded by the answer, though perhaps it was just that he didn't care. He was holding Warif's phone. It still had a charge, and Warif guessed that they must have switched it off after he'd been brought in and had only just now turned it back on. The man continued to question him, clipped inquiries in a dull, bureaucratic monotone, but his attention seemed to be focused on the device. Warif had the feeling that the fake account was about to reveal itself, point the finger at him. The man was scrolling: he opened all the apps, searched his Whatsapp messages, then went through his galleries—videos and photos both.

Warif was primed for questions about the photos but none came, because the man had now turned his attention back to the Facebook account: first the messages, then the list of posts that Warif had liked. Finally, as Warif watched in the glow from the tiny supermarket next to the building, he started to check deleted posts. Though he didn't yet have a concrete cause for concern, Warif began to feel anxious. He hadn't counted on this. Nevertheless, he stayed outwardly calm and tried to stop his left knee from moving again. Now the man gave a sigh, of relief almost.

It was a silly little post, all said and done, but as a precaution he'd deleted it from the official account. He'd posted it by accident just a few days before, forgetting to switch accounts. Just a stupid joke, deleted moments later. He'd had no idea that such posts could still be retrieved.

He'd just finished a job, taking a group around the major tourist sites. It was routine work, and he'd tried, as always, to accomplish the impossible: keeping the tourists happy while simultaneously distracting them from the chaos of the streets—the persistent shopkeepers and beggars, the petty criminality. While dissuading them from dispensing endless and ultimately ineffective bribes, he had to be ready to deal with unforeseen events: the sudden appearance of street children or school trips, random acts of verbal or physical aggression from passersby—quite apart from the standard threats of sexual harassment and theft. He wasn't working alone, but he was the only person who knew how to speak the language. His colleagues, not that there were ever more than two of them, had almost immediately vanished, off to find some shady spot to sip tea and smoke. Warif's thinning patience had finally snapped when, at the end of a particularly miserable excursion, he first noticed the heaps of garbage piled on the sidewalk outside the site, and then was approached by a couple from the group, a Black couple, who wanted him to hail a taxi so they could go off on some mission of their own. The driver he stopped had glanced with irritation, even disgust, at the couple, clearly upset that out of the group gathered on the sidewalk, it was these two he'd have to take. Not that he left any room for doubt, waving his arm at the couple and telling Warif:

"I'm not taking the Blacks. What about the others?"

In the face of this brazen ugliness, feeling that his efforts to preserve the happy ignorance of his charges from the reality of their surroundings had been effectively sabotaged, Warif exploded at the driver, who was initially mystified by this sudden anger. He assumed that Warif was trying to keep the European gold for himself, and the scene concluded with an exchange of abuse and the taxi pulling away, at which point members of his group, foremost among them the couple, wanted to know why he was so upset. Warif, calmer now with some of his anger spent and his sense of professional duty restored, told them that the driver had been trying to get an inflated fare. It didn't really explain the violent rage they'd just witnessed, but they said nothing.

Once back home, Warif had opened Facebook and written that, based on his personal experience, the only hope for the tourist industry would be if everyone, young and old, from the highest official to the lowliest trainee, plus the hawkers selling junk around the tourist traps, the hotel cleaning staff, the taxi drivers, the guys offering rides on horseback and camel hump, and, if at all possible, every single pedestrian on the street, wasn't just replaced—it wasn't a question of training or competency or basic manners, it was an issue of mentality, of culture—but substituted wholesale with citizens from other countries. What, give foreigners our jobs so they could reap the profits? It wouldn't matter, wrote Warif, because with better management, with a bit more hygiene and a little less begging and groping and harassment, and—what was more, and more important—by letting in a bit of straightforward human kindness and happiness while doing away with the religious and cultural odium directed, whether explicitly or tacitly, toward these visitors, then the sector would flourish and grow and, at last, might be equal to the country's potential as a tourist destination. Its income would be doubled many, many times over, and just the taxes on that—let's say half of it going to the state—just that fifty percent, would be many times over the country's current GDP.

Before posting, Warif added a final paragraph: *In my view, that's only a start. Honestly, there's not a single sector in the country that wouldn't do better if foreigners replaced us.* Then he put a smiley and clicked *Post*.

Because he'd just gotten home, the account open on his phone was his official one, and when, a few moments later, he realized his mistake, he'd transferred the post to his anonymous account and deleted the original. That is, until the man with the commanding voice found it and read it beneath the white neon glow of the supermarket.

"What do you mean by 'every single sector in the country should be run by foreigners'?"

Warif swallowed, his throat bone-dry from the hours spent sitting in the hallway, and attempted, without much conviction, to smile.

"Ah, it's a joke. It's not…"

The man, who Warif now realized was not as thin or as young as he'd first thought, cut him off: "A joke? What's funny about it?"

Warif tried to explain, simply, that he'd been playing, that it wasn't meant seriously, but somehow he couldn't get the point across. The man's eyes boring into him seemed to block his ability to think. He wanted to claim the smiley at the end of the post as evidence, but even that seemed unconvincing.

"You want our country to be occupied, you little prick?"

Come on now, he wanted to say, that's too much, but the derision with which one of the others said that the only foreigner he'd ever see would be the one who came to fuck him from behind, made him realize that whatever he said now, supposing he found anything to say at all, would make no difference. His fate, in that moment, was sealed for good.

The sun, suddenly flaring through a chink between two clouds, brought him back to himself. He was at the metro station next to the mausoleum of Saad Zaghloul. Once underground, he was surprised by how empty it was compared to the streets overhead. On the train, he sat opposite a young woman that he'd thought was a boy until he'd seen the small breasts barely lifting the front of her baggy shirt. Her head was totally shaved and she was barefoot. A pair of sandals rested against her canvas bag. A hippie bag, thought Warif. She looked very young. The novel in her hand was by Zola. French? From time to time she would snatch a glance at Warif, and as they braked for the next station she slipped her feet into the sandals and almost jumped onto the platform. Through the window, he saw her look at him again. Maybe she was looking at him because he was looking at her. As the train pulled away he saw her looping her arms around the neck of a boy with long hair and bare feet, and Warif thought to himself how, in their embrace, he could hardly tell them apart.

6

A BREAK FROM TWO GODS

He was looking down at the water, telling himself that Sally's feet were brushing the river's surface despite the fact that the Aboul Ela Bridge—a century-old crossing to al-Gezira, since torn down and reconstructed as a walkway running parallel to the Corniche—passed high over the waves.

About two decades before, the bridge had been decommissioned and dismantled. When they started building it again it had been like a video playing in reverse: tons and tons of broken-up metalwork reassembled, steel ornaments reaffixed, even the great lamps once installed on the bridge's stone pedestals had been dug up from where they lay in dirt and rust, rats and snakes, and mounted over the river as before, this time in a great semicircle that arced out from the Corniche where the neighborhood

Aboul Ela once stood, to rejoin it farther down. The walkway could open to let the river boats through and, when their sails were tall enough and there were people gathered on the bridge on either side, it looked like giant shark fins moving through a crowd, though the cries that greeted them were of glee, not terror, and musicians on either side of the opening would play a tune each time one went by. Sally was humming along, sitting on the edge of the bridge with her legs swinging in the air and her back resting against one of those resurrected antique lampposts. It looked so much like her feet must be dipping in that water that he couldn't resist leaning forward every now and again, as though he needed to remind himself that it couldn't be her setting the tiny eddies spinning far below.

He was beside her, propped against the barrier, hypnotized by the way the light breeze played over the rippled surface. He had the feeling that he'd been here for thousands of years, age after age passing him by as he stretched out on a green bank running down to the river, his ears soothed by the sound of music and his eyes by the sight of white ducks drifting proudly by.

These thoughts, in which time was both absent and endless, took the edge off his constant state of disorientation as he grappled with the fact that all these changes had come to pass in less time than he'd been away. The scene before him—green streets of grass, birds, impossible beauty—was so overwhelmingly present that it frequently displaced his recollection of prison, as though he'd never lived through it. But however strong the pull toward forgetting, some other part of him felt regret that these painful memories were melting away so rapidly, dispersing like a handful of dust, come and gone like a brief fever, a fleeting cramp in the stomach. He sometimes wondered if his panic attacks weren't a reaction to this, and as he considered it again now, the thought took him back to what the two tall men had said about the need for a psychological evaluation. He shook his head to clear the burgeoning anxiety that threatened to sweep him away from the here-and-now with Sally and the bridge. A new piece of music was playing now. Schubert, he thought.

From what he understood, that was unusual. The woman who'd made Sally with a European some thirty years ago could no longer remember anyone who'd come into her life in the last fifteen. Sitting out on her balcony, or in the breathtaking living room of her apartment in Heliopolis—one of the few areas where the recent changes were only visible in the population—she would sip coffee and tea and talk earnestly and enthusiastically about current events, the most recent of which had taken place back in the 1990s. Unless they'd known them personally, they couldn't hope to have heard of the great mass of the dead she mentioned in her monologues, touching them with the present tense and bringing them back from the grave. The here-and-now she described was peopled with crowds of these dead, drifting through the ghosts of events and parties, celebrations and tragedies. Alzheimer's had gotten her early, freezing her in pre-senility, and she had continued from there, living and reliving the same life for more than a decade. From time to time, she'd be bewildered to find herself addressed by a pretty young woman wearing her face and claiming to be her daughter. Both the live-in nurse and the housekeeper conspired with Sally to reduce surprises to a bare minimum, to keep her as she was: a happy woman reliving her middle years. It had therefore been most unusual—so unusual that for a fleeting moment Sally even felt something like hope—when her mother mentioned Warif's name as she sat sipping tea. How was he? She'd only met him once or twice, and those occasions had been, in her terms, relatively recent, despite lying far on the other side of all those great changes—though these changes, in respect to the period in which the mother lived, lay far in the future. Why him, though? Sally wondered. Why Warif, when Sally herself (she had no problem admitting this) had frequently forgotten him during his seemingly endless sentence?

Was it the odd name that had stuck with the old woman? Warif Shaheen. Sally used to love to tease him about it, with that cruelty she thought of as affectionate. She would tell him he didn't deserve it, so distinctive and with an almost musical lilt. He should have been a famous actor or a poet, a man of industry and wealth at the very least. She could see it blazoned across movie posters or book covers, wrapped around cans of food, but here he was (and she'd laugh): "a basic white man" in a society that had no real grasp of what that might mean. With his idleness, his lack of purpose, he'd wasted a name that his parents must have taken great pains to get right, whether they'd picked it from a list or ripped it straight from the Levantine branch of their family. Here she was with her dull, mongrel name, "Sally Adam," its double echo of her Egyptian and European genes—if she'd been as lucky as Warif she would have done everything she could to live up to it.

Whenever she got like that, got mean, he wouldn't argue, wouldn't do as he did with Wagdi and try to counter with his "perspective"—essentially a rational overview of his professional abilities, which he'd summarize as "enough to achieve my ambitions, though perhaps not my dreams" and that explained in turn his refusal to work harder to rise to meet what was, in the end, a very low ceiling. Instead, he'd ask her how many glasses of wine she'd drunk that day. Today, as she sat on the lip of the bridge, legs swinging free and laughing as though she couldn't fall, he felt that same edge in her voice. Schubert had shifted to Haydn and the number of pedestrians had swollen steadily until their chatter was a single hum harmonizing with the strings, and Warif felt strangely happy that Sally hadn't lost her mean streak, as though it was one of the few roots that remained embedded in his life.

But as she leaned back into him, asking him to lift her down off the wall, then slipped into her black shoes, and again as they walked together down the avenue of theaters where the Wakalat al-Balah market used to be, Sally was imagining other reasons her mother might have remembered him. Had she seen in Warif, perhaps, what her daughter had seen, the day she met him at the bank: the fragility she rarely encountered in the men that went for her, whether at work or the foreign cultural institutes? Even before he'd told her, she'd known he was an only child and that as a result he'd never done his national service, never experienced the obligatory rite of having one's spirit broken and remade. She had also thought she could tell, from his shyness, that he was a virgin, and that, moreover, he was trying not to show it, and so she hadn't felt the slightest trepidation as she reached out across the L-shaped sofa in the ground-floor apartment on Champollion

Street and tugged the condom off his penis.

Because she knew he was clean, and that he was anxious. She tossed the rubber across the room and pulled him onto her, taking him into her and holding him there. Years later, just after his release, she did the same, and he felt in the moment as though he was in a simulation that was repeating itself. From the outset she'd held him prisoner with her tenderness and confidence, established her sovereignty over him, but at the same time she'd seen him as a child, and would scold him like one. When her mother met him—back before she'd stepped with both feet into her time machine and finally lost all touch with the present—in the vast living room whose windows looked out over Midan Triomphe, she had surely seen the same thing. Though her mother, perhaps, had pitied him.

Sally asked him to take a photo of her beneath an olive tree whose branches reached between the glittering lights of two theaters, just a few meters before the intersection of July 26 and Galaa. She had this peculiar habit of taking photos as keepsakes that gave no hint of where they were taken: a whole file on her phone full of her face framed by trees and flowers and cats and books. They had been taken in Paris and Athens and Rome and New York, everywhere she'd traveled with her foreign passport, but not a single selfie in front of the Parthenon or

Acropolis or Pantheon, not one shot by the Eiffel Tower or the Brooklyn Bridge. It made him laugh. Just like a spy, he'd tell her: brushing over her tracks. He would test her, ask if she could remember where she'd taken this photo or that. But it also occurred to him that she saw herself as the photo's center; that there was no point in recording the place.

Recently, his own phone's gallery had been filling up as well. He'd had to get used to it, something as simple as stopping to take a photo on the street without looking over your shoulder, without anyone stopping you, without passersby staring you down. You didn't need to pretend that you were checking your messages or wait for the streets to clear or for the guards at the buildings to look away. You didn't need to have an excuse ready just to take a shot. He'd started photographing things, him with things or the things with him, and noticed that he had ended up doing exactly the same as Sally: lying back on the grass that had replaced asphalt and rubble and framing his face with dewy green lawn, or perhaps the blue-green of the Nile in a such a way that it was impossible to tell where he was. Then his approach changed, only taking photos of the city, of the neighborhoods that had grown up where the old ones had once stood. Some were selfies, but others were just buildings, the way postcards used to be. Alternating between his presence and absence in the photos paralleled, or so he'd conclude when he thought of it later, the nature of the neighborhoods themselves, both present and vanished. He felt like he was seeing his country through a visitor's eyes—the familiar strangeness of it, the need to document things as though aware of how transient their beauty was—but the places he was fondest of weren't green lanes, giant screens, or spotless trains, but rather the things that had been rescued from oblivion: the bridge he'd just been sitting on with Sally, for instance, or the villa of Umm Kulthoum, which had been pulled down then moved a few meters down the street and rebuilt exactly as it had been. He heard that they'd restored Sayyid Darwish's house at the far end of that long alleyway in Kom al-Dikka, as well, and that in this and all the other reconstructions they had employed incredible skill and expertise to ensure that they looked their age: paints whose colors came out sun-bleached, traceries of cracks worked into the pre-weathered stone. In some of them, hidden speakers in the walls played music, and holographic projections of the famous and dead moved across the windows and opened their mouths in song—all of which, Wagdi told him, had given rise to rumors of hauntings among the local population. Warif liked to go to these shrines, to poke around and fill his phone's memory with images, smiling at buildings that played the role of landmarks, as if he were playing at pilgrimage: the originals of most of these places had disappeared long before he'd been born, but here they were now, they and he together, captured in this new reality.

As they were crossing the intersection onto July 26 Street's long sweep down to Ataba, the crowd suddenly thickened around them, people on every side hurrying as though late for work. Languages ran into one another, pitched both high and low, now machine-gunning, now measured. Careless feet kept stepping on his and he was reminded of movies, crowd scenes in New York. When he glanced at Sally she had her hands buried in her overcoat's deep pockets, out of the sting of the sudden cold breeze that now cut through the mass of pedestrians. It was like she belonged to the scene, like it had been made for her, and he thought, *It was like the newcomers had brought their weather with them.* Air moved in ways it never had before; there was cold of a sort he'd never felt before. Maybe it was just his memory at fault. On his right loomed the dark hulk of the Supreme Court, faintly washed by the spotlights at the base of its Italianate, century-old pillars; on the left, branching off the side of the road where the market for old car parts used to sprawl, were a line of alley mouths, each terminating in a lit entryway—more theaters, perhaps. No sign, though, of the historic cinema on the corner just before Alfi Street where he and Wagdi had once ridden pillion on a motorcycle. The driver asked them for a push start, and when he shouted back to offer them a ride, maybe not even in earnest, they jumped on laughing and he took them to a café down one of the alleys that led off the square. It was the only time Warif had ever been on a motorbike.

They crossed the road at Talaat Harb. The crowds thinned, and to his surprise he found his legs getting tired. This was why he'd taken a shortcut through the tunnel back to the Corniche after meeting the unplaceable man in Hoda Shaarawi. He glanced sideways as he crossed at the intersection of Sharif and Adly, and found himself remembering that, as the pair of officers had pulled him past this same spot seven years before, he'd been trying to remember phone numbers—Sally's or Wagdi's or even his father's, who might have been giving himself a shot of insulin at that very moment—and how later, watching other detainees dropping scraps of paper with their relatives' numbers out of the windows, he'd told himself that no one living in a country like this could afford the luxury of not memorizing such details. All he saw now was a crowd clustered around an ice-cream stand. Cold as it was, they were licking and chatting and joking. And where he'd once crossed the road with the men, there was a long conga line of young people, coupled like train cars as they pushed through the mob all singing together, raucous as drunks. Catching him staring, Sally asked if he wanted ice cream, and he found himself grinning. She slipped behind him, and just as he thought she must be going to straighten his spine, he felt her jump on his back and wrap herself around him, arms over his shoulders, legs around his waist. He staggered and they almost fell. She was laughing. The weight, and the suddenness of the assault, forced a groan out of him, and with a quick "Sorry" she slid off. "Is your back okay? I'm an idiot…" she began, her voice trailing off, but he could hear her thoughts, worrying about what the years in prison might have done to his back. The truth though, the astonishing truth, was that nothing had happened, or not to his back, despite the overcrowded prisoner transport, despite the shackles, despite (this the true miracle) the wooden board that had been both a makeshift cover for the latrine and his bed. His genes, or at least the bones and flesh nurtured on thousands of his mother's stews and his father's bread, this body that was his only inheritance from Shaheen and Naela, had remained intact through those seven years. Even what he'd tried to do to his mind—those repeated attempts embarked on with cold deliberation—had come to nothing; maybe no surprise given that his mind, a product of the cells in his gray brain bouncing off each other, was part of that same body.

Standing next to Sally on the corner of Sharif Street, he tried persuading himself that he should be happy; happy to see the streets full of life at last, free to be walked along without fear even though those who walked them might be different. Look: the khedival buildings made like new, with the shine that once had vied with Europe's fully restored. The sunlight gleaming off their domes could be seen from the windows of the apartment in Famm al-Khaleej. Years ago now, back when he was still working, a tourist told him that the route they walked down—Suleiman Pasha, Qasr al-Nil, and Sabry Abu Alam, then circling the statue of Talaat Pasha Harb to see it from every angle—reminded her of the main street to a city square in her home country. That's what she'd claimed, even though it was still chaos back then, the sidewalks full of garbage and beggars, littered with vendors who, permanently camped out by their wares, still claimed to be itinerant. What would she say if she could see the streets as they are now? he wondered. Then thought that she could indeed be somewhere in the crowd around him, not so different from himself, in fact, with his barely Egyptian features and, most importantly, with Sally: a passport that either preempted, or carried him discreetly past, all obstacles. The people who'd lived here before he went to prison were happily installed in their new neighborhoods. They were calmer now, their futures more secure. He himself had seen the money his father left him reassume its worth with the influx of newcomers, buoyed by a resurgent currency, as had his bank bond, the sole investment he'd made before they'd taken him away: a slip of paper plumping and growing as its owner courted madness in his cell. If he'd done as his contemporaries had and taken the pension—the payout to give up his job—or even Wagdi's offer of a local salary for a local job, then everything would turn out fine, at least in theory. But he wanted his old job back for too many reasons to count. One of them—he now realized, gazing at her as she stood motionless amid the passing crowds, gazing back at him—was that if he didn't, Sally would, irretrievably, belong to another world.

"Why did we stop?" Sally asked. A question that would be better addressed to his aching knees.

"Come on," she said, "we don't want to be late."

They were on their way to meet friends of hers at Shepheard's Hotel, resurrected on its old site on Opera Square fronting the recently expanded Ezbekiya Gardens, which had enveloped the National Theater and the Brides' Theater in a lush green that spilled north two-thirds of the length of Gaish Street and westward to the park around

Abdeen Palace. She wanted him to meet her friends, she'd said. He needed to "rejoin life" and "meet people," maybe the only phrases she'd uttered without invoking her gods of cruelty and irony, a dyad she frequently syncretized into a single deity. Unusual in itself, her invitation took on even greater significance precisely because he knew she would go on living her own life regardless, with or without him, and more often without.

He couldn't stop seeing it, though, the line that started from the intersection where he'd crossed to buy those cigarettes seven years ago, snaking up Adly Street. It was like a wall cutting through the crowds, between the laughter and ice-cream eaters, the cars quietly waiting at the traffic lights in neat rows. And as he looked, his knees pressed backward and locked, a cold sweat pricked his forehead, and he thought he would rather be anywhere but here.

Just then another cloud of pedestrians engulfed him, and for a moment he lost sight of Sally. As the sweat poured and his heart beat harder he felt as though a crack had opened in the sidewalk between them and he was falling in. More alarming still was the fact that even the presence of all these people didn't keep the fear at bay, and once again he was reminded that a person dies alone. Then the laughter and chatter, the music thudding out of shop doors, faded away and the crowd parted to reveal

Sally coming toward him. She laid a hand on his shoulder and asked him if he was all right. There were other voices, too, he realized to his surprise, a blend of accents all asking him the same thing. The panic inside of him must have leaked out, been seen. He felt ashamed, then angry, which proved effective in pulling him out of the hole, but all the same he told Sally that he wanted to go home, refusing her offer to accompany him. She must have been thinking how weak he was, but he didn't care. He told her to go on; he'd walk back alone. In his head he was sketching out the wide, looping line he needed to follow if he was to keep clear of the walls that sprouted up wherever he looked, or the cracks that branched out beneath his feet.

He reached the cover of the dense tangle of acacias and banyans along the Garden City Corniche before he felt calm. Winter had felled what leaves survived the autumn, and the bare branches overhead were a snarl of skeletal limbs. He looked out at the Nile, its waters black beyond the yellow lamps that ran along the line of the almost-deserted pathway, their light catching nothing but dust and gnats. He was in a bad way, he realized, and called Wagdi, inviting him over when he finished work.

By the time Wagdi arrived Warif had already drunk a great deal. Why didn't Wagdi write something about the cracks appearing all over Downtown, he wanted to know? Suddenly the paving stones would crack, the ground would split open, and if you didn't watch out you could fall to your death.

They were on the balcony, watching the woods that carpeted the place where the Zeinhom neighborhood had once stood. Wagdi didn't interrupt, just sipped wine and smoked, but when Warif was done, he smiled and said that they didn't cover the areas where the newcomers lived, but he'd certainly make a note of the suggestion. Then he asked Warif if he'd been with Sally.

Even in the depths of his drunkenness, Warif was still alive to the fact that Wagdi didn't like Sally much, that he thought she was a bad influence. Who was Wagdi to judge a relationship like theirs anyway? Just his oldest friend… He chuckled to himself then realized that he hadn't answered the question. Yes, of course, but Sally wasn't the cause of *this*, if there was a single cause to begin with. Better to change the subject:

"You seen all those excavators at the end of the street? There are more of them every day."

Wagdi saw the attempted sidetrack and went with it. "God help us, hey?"

"God help your mother most of all."

From the cold balcony their laughter rose up on clouds of red wine, brandy, and tobacco smoke.

From the mobile phone he'd left on the arabesque coffee table in the living room, he heard the ping of a message coming in. He didn't need to get up and look to know what it said.

7

DECK OF CARDS

At first, Warif thought the room was empty. He was used to the blinding light that always accompanied these meetings, but this time he could see where it was coming from, flooding through the big window and making the white furniture glow. There was no desk this time, just a sofa up against the wall that faced the window and next to it, at a slight angle, a chair of the same design, broad and deep, its cupped back inviting slumber. Warif hadn't even noticed the woman sitting in the chair, so small she almost vanished into it, and white as well, impossibly pale in the palest clothes; the whole scene seemed to have been designed as an optical illusion. She welcomed him in a soft, accented voice, and asked him to sit on the sofa.

There being no desktop to hold them, there

were of course no devices, no computer or phone or printer, and the only table in the room, a sort of translucent stand by the lefthand arm of the sofa, was also empty. Nor was the woman holding anything. The encounter felt entirely circumstantial, like sharing a bench at a train station or the glassy impersonality of a space station. But the woman knew his name. In fact, she knew everything: age, sex, place of birth, even his medical records—everything was stored away in that neat head perched on a slender neck, its necklace glinting in the light. If it wasn't for the vestige of human warmth she gave off, he would have said he was in the presence of a machine.

Had it been easy to find his way here, she wanted to know, as though speaking to an old friend. Warif nodded. It was perhaps too soon to start a discussion about what the word "easy" might mean. The building in question, on one of whose upper floors the office was located, overlooked the al-Hussein mosque. But something felt out of place, because he could also see the al-Azhar mosque from the same window just by turning his head, which suggested that he must be standing directly above the Bab al-Ghouriya neighborhood—only the neighborhood was still there, transformed into an open-air museum. Warif told himself that from such a height, a height hinted at somehow by the sheer volume of light pouring through the window, a person might well feel they were anywhere.

Despite the softness of her voice and the delicacy of the throat that produced it, despite that ineffable human warmth, the woman spoke with a cut-glass clarity that filled the room's broad sweep:

"Looking through your file, Mr. Warif, I notice repeated references to your involvement in what happened, that the current situation was somehow a proposal of yours. Would that be correct? Let me rephrase that: Do you believe that to be correct?"

He had an answer ready for her, but her rephrasing made him pause. What did she mean by "believe"?

It was as though she'd anticipated what he was going to say. It's very important, she said, not to be too quick to accept at face value anything said by people who had experienced extended periods of incarceration. Regardless of how pleasant the conditions of that incarceration might have been. Not that pleasant is how she would characterize his time in prison, she added, and her voice seemed tinged with sorrow. Well, besides the last few months…

"After the storm, you mean."

"Precisely. After the sandstorm. They say it was the worst of times, but that it brought the best in its wake! Apologies if I sound like I'm giving a pep talk, but that's right, isn't it? Anyway, back to my question."

It took Warif a couple of seconds to remember what the question was, and as he pondered it he unthinkingly reached out toward the side table to pick up a drink that wasn't there.

"Can I get you something? Water?"

He shook his head, took a breath, and answered, "It would be an exaggeration to say what happened was 'my idea.' Lots of people thought the same thing."

"But it all began exactly the way you wrote it. That's what I'm told."

"Looks like you're trying to persuade me."

She shrugged. "Not at all." There was silence, then she continued, "The fact is, there are others, just a few people, who made similar suggestions about other things. And as far as we can tell, their circumstances are much like your own."

He was on the verge of asking why they were having this meeting at all, which had started out like a psychologist's examination and was now shading into a police interview, but now her words took him back to that time following the street abduction and the long wait in the hall: the period after they brought him to the dark entryway of that building on the corner of Sharif and Talaat Harb, when the room had emptied of everyone but himself and one other young man who was squatting on a long, low slab that protruded from the wall opposite Warif. A ribbon of light was falling through a gap in the iron of the Italianate gate and across the man's eyes.

What Warif remembered after that was like a montage, cuts and jumps seen out of the corner of his eye or through a slip of the T-shirt that was his blindfold. And the smells. The vest he wore, which carried the scent of Sally's perfume until it was blotted out by the flat metallic reek of the microbus seats beneath which his head was pressed, then the rusty funk in the crowded truck where he was propped against people rather than side panels, all blindfolded and banging against the sides, swaying around at random, lurching into one another and slamming against the walls, suddenly realizing that they couldn't breathe and panicking, drumming against the metal as their blindfolds loosened and slid. And then the response, a grinding hum like a giant fan turning, then another, powerful smell, acrid, accompanied by the sensation of the stinging spray that settled in the creases of the closed eyes like chili dust till they wept like children, wept despite themselves till they were too tired to cry and there was a silence during which Warif thought he must be dead. He remembered all this, but this wasn't it, the thing that this petite, translucent woman was summoning with her words.

They transferred them to a second truck (smaller, he assumed, but maybe that was only because it was more crowded, though maybe it was both smaller *and* more crowded) where they waited for more than twenty-four hours. Warif wouldn't have believed that a person could stay like that for all that time: a canned sardine, held upright only by the bodies packed around it, preserved in a miasma of sweat and fear. During those hours and hours crammed in the truck, a new and unfamiliar sensation took root in him, something he felt with his body but that was unable, maybe due to the tight press, to reach his mind. Or maybe it was because, for most of that time, his mind was fully preoccupied with a desperate need to piss. Fortunately, someone eventually passed him a little plastic bottle, whose mouth he slipped through his fly. He thumbed in the head of his penis and was able to at least partially relieve himself. Maybe that would help him shrink a little, he thought; maybe it might win him a little more space.

When at last the door opened and he saw through the rapidly disintegrating weave of the cheap local cotton the others climbing out, the strange feeling returned; he felt it even as he staggered through the opening and his head scraped the side. He looked back and saw more climbing down, a seemingly never-ending line, as though the truck was a portal, pulling people from some parallel dimension.

But the nature of that strange feeling, he only later began to understand, however vaguely, once the strangeness had built up and assumed the form of a single, embodied truth—though even then it was still hard to grasp. When they took him and a few others from the blindfolded huddle and pushed them into a basement where they sat for a few more hours, he was almost ashamed of the happiness that swept through him just to be in a room with a handful of unoccupied floor tiles on which he might stretch himself out. In the light that filtered down from a peephole set high in the door he half-imagined he saw things moving over the floor: tiny, colorless creatures. But he and his companions all laid down regardless, and the creatures vanished beneath their bodies. When they moved him again, from that room to another truck then to another room, and finally out into a long corridor—lit this time by actual lightbulbs, albeit caked in dust—he saw (past the blindfold that was now little more than a rag) something that brought the feeling back.

At first, he'd thought that the other detainees must be foreigners, but once he saw their body language and caught the few words that were uttered the notion was dispelled. A few moments later, when he looked up at the young man sitting across from him on the other side of the corridor, he had the fleeting impression that he was looking into a mirror. The man was almost identical to him; only the clothes were different. Then in a sudden flash of understanding, delayed no doubt by the fact he hadn't eaten for hours, Warif realized that, fat and thin, old and young, everyone sitting in that corridor resembled him in some way. Everyone had the same pale skin as he did, the aquiline nose and slightly receding chestnut hair. They were like a family gathering, say, or the surviving members of a defeated tribe rounded up and locked away, and it was at this precise moment that he grasped the true shape of the strangeness he'd felt in that crowded truck. Everyone in that truck, even those who hardly looked like him at all (to the extent that he could see them) scraped the top of the doorframe with their heads as they'd stumbled out. There was no tall or short: everyone was exactly the same height.

Later on, they were given something to eat: a few grams of beans or a shaving of sweet sesame paste on a disc of stale bread. The food sharpened his awareness, made him more conscious of the patterns in each place they were brought to: the cells and passageways, the crowded trucks; the way their heads stood the same distance to the roofs of those trucks, the way they shared the same quasi-foreign features. Later, he was held with another group. These didn't look like him, though he still felt that he'd seen them somewhere before; in fact, he remembered one as a childhood friend from Old Cairo, and after a few whispered consultations, they all realized that they'd been born in that same neighborhood. Later still, elsewhere, he overheard a conversation in Russian between a couple of men on the far side of the room, and this time he discovered that everyone in the cell was either a graduate of, or studying in, a language department. It made him feel like one card among many, that he was being shuffled in the deck with all the rest. Anyway, none of that, curious as it was, was what he wanted to talk about now, not with this pale woman in this white office.

One cell had been bigger than the rest. It smelled of dust and was lit by a window (had it been a window?) that ran the full width of the wall but was only a few centimeters high. Sometimes the light seemed cool and electric, sometimes it looked like sunlight, but maybe it was two neon bars alternating, one blue, one yellow. From time to time, the cement floor would tremble, as though some massive vehicle was rumbling past not far away. He'd feel it run through his body and it would seem as though everyone else in the room was trembling too, a faint, shared shudder, like the worshippers he'd seen as a boy when his mother would take him to the shrine of Morsi Aboul Abbas. By now almost all the blindfolds had ridden up, fallen off, or fallen apart. The long, thin window cast a stripe of light over the bodies and the rare patch of bare cement. Warif realized he was barefoot. Like in one of those nightmares where you forget some essential article of clothing. He could scarcely remember what shoes he'd been wearing. Maybe the running shoes he'd bought a year ago in Maadi, from that shop half-hidden behind a tree? He'd hoped they might finally persuade him to commit to regular exercise. Or was it the brown leather clompers whose weight lent a solidity to his stride, their tapping soles a boost to his self-confidence? Regardless, right now he couldn't feel his feet.

Maybe it was the size of the cell, maybe the fact he was held there for longer, or just the monotonous regularity of everything in there—the steady rod of light, the soft repeated quakes, the blindfolds falling apart—that set a thread of whispers stringing out between the inmates. This time it was less clear what they had in common. It wasn't the way they looked or their height, it had nothing to do with the way they spoke or dressed or where they came from—but then the kid sitting against the gray wall next to Warif, who hadn't stopped asking him questions in a low, anxious voice, as though he thought Warif might be a police officer himself, declared at last, querulously, that he'd only made a suggestion… Just a simple suggestion, inspired by his recent return from working abroad: that people make the effort to smile at citizens returning to Egypt. That was it. That the airport staff and passport officers and customs agents crack a smile. But had he made a joke about it? Warif asked. Possibly. And did the joke go viral, did people share it? Maybe, they might have, but all he'd wanted was the best for his country. Right? He was asking the question as though his fate rode on Warif's answer. Right? A little later, a second man, who still had a sandal on one foot, murmured that he'd only said the sidewalks needed to be widened, regardless of the buildings that might have to be knocked down. Regardless of the buildings? And what might he mean by that? His interrogator had wanted to know. It reminded Warif of when the younger officer had asked him what he meant by "every single sector in the country," and now he understood the thing that bound them together, here in the big cell with its blue and yellow light: from every corner the suggestions came in—smart and stupid, derisive and serious, plausible and impossible, imported from overseas and proudly homegrown.

One of them asked Warif what suggestion had brought him there, a question that, if it weren't for the circumstances in which they found themselves, might have made him smile. He assured the man that their suggestions couldn't be responsible, but the involuntary tremor in his voice told him that he wasn't as sure as he sounded.

He was starting to see the woman more clearly now, able to differentiate her paleness from the whites of the light and furniture and walls. She said that he must have noticed, of course, how after they transferred him to a new cell following the sandstorm—not to mention after he got out!—the changes that had taken place were a more-or-less identical, albeit amplified, version of the post he'd made seven years before. But Warif, always careful to maintain his native skepticism, and never one to promote himself, insisted on giving coincidence its due. Once more conscious of the complete absence of any form of refreshment on the table beside him, he said that he sometimes thought about the people who'd shared that last cell with him, that whenever he noticed a change out here he would recall…well, not their faces, given how poorly lit the place was, but their voices, their suggestions. Only, just as he'd say of his own, he wouldn't say that the vast majority of the proposals he heard, no matter how wild or absurd they might have been, could properly be described as original in any meaningful way. They must have occurred to other people before that; even the most complex and ingenious were obvious enough if you bothered to think about it.

It was true that some of things he saw—like the parachute jumps that tourists took from a platform atop the Muqattam cliffs down to the rolling parks that covered the old City of the Dead—did bear an uncannily detailed resemblance to things he'd heard. That one in particular had been raised during an endless murmured conversation that afterward had seemed to him like a long dream; when later he saw the parachutists it shook his conviction in coincidence. But then again, while he could remember that detail, he couldn't remember what it was about the suggestion that would plausibly explain why its proponent was in prison. He'd tried, but he couldn't remember: all he saw was a pair of pale eyes—pale because gray, and gray, maybe, due to the light—and all he heard was a voice that had reminded him strongly of an old friend from primary school, though the man was certainly much younger.

The woman was listening, seemed almost to be sharing his memories of the place, but her next comment completely derailed his train of thought:

"I'm not sure that taking the suggestions as the reason for your detention is quite the right way to look at it. It might be more accurate to say that those who made suggestions were among those detained, that they constituted one category of prisoners among others."

A pause, then Warif slowly nodded, remembering

all the groups he had been a part of: height and appearance, education and origin. But behind these thoughts, another: What did any of that have to do with him being here today, with this woman? Before he could give voice to his confusion, something occurred to him: "But most of the changes, whether it was coincidence or not, happened after you all arrived."

The woman looked flatly at him without answering, as though she didn't quite understand what he'd said. He tried again, "I mean, if there's something to the theory—if there's some connection between all those people gathered into a single cell and everything that later happened outside—then you, which is to say the newcomers, would have something to do with it. But how can there be a connection, seeing as you hadn't arrived yet?"

The merest shadow of a smile passed over her face. "Let's say we try to take advantage of every available opportunity." Then, quickly, before he could say anything in response, she added, "But what matters to me now is whether you've told me everything you have to say. Is there anything you might have omitted from this period? Not just your time in that one cell: I mean the whole seven years."

It took Warif a while to find his answer.

"I think you know everything, to be honest."

"There's always that one thing we aren't able to

find out."

He shook his head. "Nothing that matters. I was a prisoner like any other."

"And it's true? You want to go back to your old job?" she asked, lifting her pale eyes to his.

He'd already answered the question so often that this time he simply nodded.

"You do know that there's already someone else doing your old job? Right?"

8

A WHITE DARK

The roar of the dark winter sea couldn't drown the sound of Sally's laughter as Warif haltingly put words to what he was feeling, the impression he had that they were sitting on the edge of the ocean.

"Isn't ocean a bit grand for the Alexandria seafront?"

She laughed again. They'd missed their appointment at the university and had decided to stay overnight at a hotel and try again in the morning. After a huge meal of grilled fish on one of the stone terraces of the Qaithey Citadel they'd gone back to the hotel, built on a spit that licked out into the sea like a tongue.

As she laughed, and with the water seemingly all around him and the stars of Alexandria overhead, Warif was trying to express how he felt. The feeling had taken shape as first they'd sat on the shore then walked down the Corniche where all the life that had built up there over the years, the nightclubs and arcades, the private rooms, the dark corners beneath bridges, even the garages, had been swept away, their absence making way for the wide spread of the winter sea, vast and domineering and violent. Its great gray half-hoop had seemed to wrap round him, like he was on an island, or sitting on one of the world's many edges: he imagined himself tasting Atlantic salt somewhere on the coast in Casablanca, or sprawled on Californian sand, staring at the Pacific. Not that he'd visited either: on his one trip overseas, eons ago now, the one where he looked through the window of the sports center at night, he'd spent a morning by the ocean, watching its waters falling away to the south. That ocean had been wild, and it had felt like he was on the roof of the world.

Now, he was looking north from Alexandria into a sea that was recovering its power. A safe distance from the water line there was a sprinkling of beach huts and small hotels; a few of the old peeling facades were still visible, but by some mysterious process they had been shifted back behind the new builds. The only thing that hadn't changed was the scarcity of people out and about on such a stormy day; even so, even from where he sat on the lip of his imagined ocean, it was easy for Warif to tell that the newcomers made up the overwhelming majority.

He had received a final piece of advice from the pale woman—that he should "get himself ready, in case"—and with support from Wagdi and with Sally's enthusiastic encouragement, he'd decided to travel north to Alexandria to get his degree certificate from the university. Before arriving, he had an image in his mind of how it would be with its old splendors restored, a naive vision dictated by a nostalgia for the city's lost character, its Greek, Italian, and Armenian past; he saw himself going to dances, watching locals dance sirtakis and kocharis, even joining in between glasses of arak instead of beer, ouzo instead of wine. That was the dream in his head that rested against the passenger-side window of Sally's car as she drove down the silky strip of asphalt that ran all the way to Alexandria. Two uninterrupted hours down the silk road, dreaming his dream of an Alexandria that swirled and stepped to the strains of Greek and Roman tunes. But it was nothing like that.

Most of the investment here seemed to be Asian, the outlets and eateries modeled after the trim, neatly ordered little buildings that fringe beaches throughout the archipelagos of the Far East. But whether residents or tourists, the newcomers here seemed to come from some of the coldest places on the planet, the far north, to whose natives an Alexandrian winter was spring. He did spot a few Americans, true, but only a few; he told himself that the tourists were held at bay by the strong January winds—that these winds, once known as the Epiphany storms, were helping protect the city's folkloric, Mediterranean identity, keeping it unspoiled throughout the rest of the year. In any case, Sally had promised he'd see some Greek faces tomorrow, when they were to tour the undersea glass tunnel that snaked through the ruins of the drowned Ptolemaic city by Abu Qir.

When he'd told her about his conversation with the pale woman, she'd said, "What, you thought they'd keep your chair empty?"

The expression made him smile—"your chair," like he was a minister or something—but even so, despite the faint sting of her sarcasm, the fact was that yes, that was exactly what he'd thought. His exact thought as he sat in darkened cells, or in corridors that blazed with light, dreaming without even closing his eyes, indifferent to the barely perceptible cycle of day or night, his sleep and waking rolled into a single state.

Sometimes, instead of visions of his apartment or his parents, instead of dreams of long wordless evenings with Wagdi, or even of Sally herself, he'd see the chair, sitting empty in the silent office, filmed with dust, rocking almost imperceptibly to the drumming of the antique floor-mounted air conditioner. Then he'd see all those colleagues he'd never quite befriended, strolling back and forth past the office, their conversations practically inaudible and unintelligible, not even noticing he was gone. Or, say, acting as though his absence was the product of some standard bureaucratic process, so utterly unremarkable: seven years unpaid leave somewhere where the light is either always on or off. The North Pole?

Some nights, sitting with his back to the wall and his knees pressed to his chest, waiting for Sally to return after another long absence, he'd think back to that trip up to the roof of the world, where the sun worked hard for six straight months then ceded its chair to night for the six that followed. A fact he'd known before he went, but it was only up there that he realized that the north's endless day, its six months of sun, wasn't exactly what you'd call a day—or if it was, then a lackluster one, lazy, hardly working at all. It had been a fleeting visit, but one day he'd been out and about and had run into a crowd of locals. There were long lines of schoolchildren dancing along to street musicians playing guitars, and everyone was heading to where the only rays of sunshine shone, a few old blocks in the commercial center, where it filtered through the bare crowns of trees, their leaves shed in anticipation of the snows to come, and illuminated a slice of street, picking out its relief and painting it—this, Warif was seeing for the first time during his visit—in its true colors. Everyone was there, young and old, happy and miserable, despairing and full of hope, ailing and healthy, crowded into that line of light. Later, on YouTube, he'd learn that the night was similarly lax, that failing to exert its full darkness, it allowed the northern lights and great clusters of stars to mock the streetlights' puny glow.

His powers of recall sometimes astonished him. He could remember it all—the world's curved roof, the cold and the bright lines of schoolkids twirling in the sun's rays—even as he sat huddled in the insufficiency of his cramped and baking cell, just two meters by one point five, where all of a sudden he would see the sand's grains jostling and jostled by the heads of the insects and then by the minutes and seconds, which were taking shape as bubbles, bubbles he could poke and pop with his fingers but that just kept coming, which seemed as if they were never meant to end. And he'd see the empty, dusty chair, too, and he'd tell himself that thirty years from now, when everyone was dead and gone, he'd return and pat that seat down, softly, softly so as not to split it, and the dust would take flight, so he'd open the window whose sill was almost level with the floor. The air conditioner would be broken, but he wouldn't need it because cold winter would have come to stay forever. He would sit in his chair, waiting as he made new memories out of the old and erasing everything that had taken place between them, and when he'd gotten his fill he would rise to his feet, taking his time, and go to see what was outside.

That's how the thoughts used to come, during the years in that narrow grave, and that's how they came to him now, their force redoubled by inertia, like the waves the sea unthinkingly tossed out along the reborn shoreline of Cleopatra. This stream of consciousness wasn't something he'd learned to do exactly, he hadn't willed himself to think this way; what he'd sought, in fact, after seemingly endless years between those baking walls, the thousands of nightmares in which, every time, the terrifying men heaved him off his mattress and dragged him away from his mother's screams and the silence of his neighbors' bolted windows—what he'd really sought so desperately, weeping for it in his solitude, bending his whole will until at last he'd touched it, was madness. This is the thing he'd kept from the pale woman.

It was his companion who'd first suggested it to him. He had watched the man, sitting with his back against the wall opposite, not understanding how the tiny space had grown to hold them both, and thought that he was maybe one of the detainees from the corridor or the crowded truck, one of the group who'd looked like him, because he was roughly

Warif's height and build. At least, that's what he assumed at first, because this was during a time when everything was very dark indeed, with only a faint glow of electric light coming from a little hole high up in the door. He never moved: back against the wall, knees to his chest, his once-white clothes shadowed by filth and darkness and despair. Did the man ever speak? There were times he thought they'd had a conversation, then he'd reconsider and tell himself they hadn't, but he was never quite sure because every fresh thought erased the last, a gradual subsiding, slipping down through a chain of dreams. Then he wondered if he was looking at himself, seeing himself across the cell as he used to do as a child adrift in daydreams, back when the cats on the stairwell would answer his questions, when the chickens on the roof would fall silent as he wandered into their world to see the neighbors leaping off from their rooftops, floating down to land, smiling, on their feet, and the bedroom wall would turn into a mirror in which he saw himself, clearly mirrored back, flexing his childish muscles or trying to catch sight of the words as they left the lips of his silent reflection. But just as he would persuade himself that it was himself he saw reflected in the cell wall, the figure would vanish, crumbling into dust then darkness. He found himself grinning as he tried to calculate how many days he'd kept him company.

A rarity, this question about time. Time, in turn, was breaking down and blowing away but enough of its sense remained for him to feel, finally, that he understood the meaning of a phrase that had puzzled him when he'd first encountered it. He had been translating a piece on physics, years ago now, back when he was trying to make translation something more than mere work: "The end of the beginning." Even now he didn't fully understand it in an intellectual sense; rather, he felt himself dissolving into that timelessness, saturated with darkness. There had been a time—was it days ago? Months? Years?—that he'd paid close attention to the frequency with which the food was slid through the hatch at the bottom of the door. He'd kept track of the days through infinitesimal variations in the bowls of wheat and barley slop, their fats and proteins—the bare minimum required to keep his organs ticking over, his mind alert enough to supervise the body's work. Then he realized that it was this that tormented him. In marking the days and counting the nights, his mind was creating hope then lacerating him with disappointment, battering him with memories, and there was no need for it. If he couldn't physically scoop the gray matter out of his head then he could at least let it crumble away, vanish into the featureless blackness, or melt into the fierce heat of the lights that burned unceasingly and turned everything a white dark. His body was clearly the stubborn kind, its gears and levers unshaken by the hammer blows of prison and the anvil of time; well, perhaps with that same willfulness, fortified by despair, he might be able to drive himself to madness. A kind of agency; a final victory over time.

He'd once read—had he translated it?—that brain activity spikes at night. In the white dark of the cell, in the irregular transitions between nightmare and waking, night and day had no meaning. Symptoms of a deteriorating mental state: a reduced awareness of one's immediate environment; an increasingly frequent inability to stay focused on a single line of thought (sometimes at least, at others an inability to escape it); and of course—and here, he cracked a smile—introversion and physical inactivity. He displayed them all, he *was* them. Some of them, in fact, he was pretty sure he exhibited before he got here, and these were what had cut his life off at the pass, producing a weakness that Sally liked to imply was there even when she wasn't openly stating it. He would have to tell her about it, maybe even ask her opinion: a last goodbye before the final departure.

He waited till she came. She sat in the same spot as his vanished twin, knees to her chest, a short skirt pulled back off her thighs. He didn't ask what she thought of the idea of giving in to madness, not directly, just whether she thought it would work. And she nodded, shot him a look of encouragement and maybe of pity, too. That was when he believed he could do it, and he wanted to ask her what she knew about madness, but the words came out in a mumble, like they did in his nightmares, so he stopped and tried again, only this time, it cost him too much to even bring the words up. But then inside him something began to glow. A sort of hope opened up. It might go quicker than he'd thought, he told himself. Caught up in the thrill of a beginning, he imagined himself with an axe in hand, roaming around his mind and laying waste: brain cells and dreams, networks of pain and pleasure alike. He wanted to hear the wind rushing unobstructed over its tumbled pillars and ruined walls. Almost immediately, he realized that memory, tricky and mutable by its very nature, posed the most serious risk to his mission. He started to think of his memories as little insects and to crush them underfoot, and as he did so, the images in his head would wink out one by one: going with his father as a little boy to watch a football match, wearing the colored paper sunhat his father had bought him; his mother taking him to school on the day of his first test, smoothing her hand over his chest before she turned him over to the teacher with tears running down his face; lying on the floor half-asleep as his neighbor stepped over him and seeing up her robe; behind his building with Noha, the neighbors' daughter, learning how soft breasts really were; the fight with the kids from the next neighborhood over, when the length of hosepipe whipped across his face and hurt so much he thought the skin was peeling off his skull; his father again, wheeling onto their street with the new bicycle that he'd been waiting for; his mother again, darning in a blackout by candlelight; himself in the instant he'd read his degree results and been overwhelmed by a feeling of emptiness; his heart drumming in his ears when he met Sally for the first time. He stared at the spot where his twin had sat, but Sally was gone. Off on some mission of her own, leaving him to complete his alone.

Had anyone ever had the same idea? More pertinently: Had anyone ever pulled it off, driving themselves crazy? There must have been many people over the shameful course of human history who had wanted it and tried, but had they succeeded? Were they all around us, perhaps, only we couldn't tell them apart from those who'd inadvertently lost their minds?

The problem, clearly, was how you defined the goal. Once someone had crossed over, so to speak, wouldn't it be impossible to get a helpful answer out of them? That didn't just go for the clinically identified, but also for the free-range cases, the mad you found at home or on the street, in buses and offices and prisons. But soon enough, he stopped asking that or any other question, because he didn't want any questions or answers cutting rational paths through the tangled chaos of his mind. Drawing on the madness, hitherto latent, generated by his solitary confinement, he started to leave his meals untouched; without engaging in a formal strike, he persuaded himself that hunger was the surest way to damage himself. Then he thought "fake it till you make it" might work, so began talking to the walls and floors, holding out hope of hearing them reply with the same determination he'd brought to bear in his boyhood conversations with pets and toys and ghosts. He sang and screamed until his throat was raw and he felt cement flakes raining from the walls. He kept his eyes shut in the light and opened them when it was dark, and used his nails to try to climb the walls, muttering threats at the ceiling: I'll get you. He lay motionless on the floor for days at time, a dead man. The puddled damp on the floor became sweet to him, and he lapped at it like a dog. He gave himself new names in English and Latin, in Ancient Egyptian, in languages both real and imagined. He addressed his father as a son and scolded his mother like a wife. He watched himself murder a man and bury the body beneath the cement floor, then cry the man's name and weep with remorse. He argued with people he'd never met and never would, filled with a genuine rage at what they said—which was one of his more successful attempts, but he could never feel proud, because in madness there was no meaning to success or failure, nor even space to consider the difference. None of which he told the pale woman, because whether a psychological evaluation or a bureaucratic procedure, nothing about their meeting seemed to encourage it.

Of course, he didn't need to tell Sally, because he already had, when she'd given him that half-encouraging, half-pitying look, knees pressed to her breasts and her back resting against the wall where his vanished twin had rested before. He often had trouble disentangling what he'd told her during her visits to his cell and what he'd said on the outside—whether after his release or before they'd pulled him in—but he decided he wouldn't bother; he'd leave it up to her to ask the questions if she felt the need.

She was questioning him now, as it happened.

They were heading back to the little hotel where they had taken separate rooms. Thanks to sweeping changes in the tourism laws, they could have shared; it was just that Sally didn't like the way he cried out in his sleep. These cries, unlike the ones he used to make before, he could never remember, as if there were some virus in his nightmares that wiped them when he woke. Anyway, they were walking when Sally asked whether the woman (she didn't call her pale, because he'd left that part out) had told him the name of the person who'd taken his job. Their nationality perhaps?

He hadn't asked, he said. It wasn't like he'd been the minister of tourism: Why would anyone know who'd replaced him?

She raised her voice against the sound of the waves that pursued them the length of the white path. "But I'm sure she knows. She told you about it, remember?"

She patted his shoulder:

"Leave it to me."

And though she didn't add "as usual," he heard it fill the silence as beneath his gaze, beneath starlight and sea spray, she turned right down a path that led to her room at the far end of the hotel. Suddenly, he remembered the painting in the office of the unplaceable man, the three women on the shore. But there was no one on the shore now. His own room was to the left. The path was deserted, nothing to see but sea and the lights in the sky. For a moment, he wondered if he was having another of his visions. He imagined himself trying to open the door to his room only to find it locked, and then waking dejected in his bed back in Cairo, or opening his eyes in terror somewhere far, far worse, and he trembled at the thought.

9

THE BIRD ON THE ROOF

Warif was shivering as they arrived at the university the next morning. There was no sign of the cart where twenty years before he'd bought sandwiches between lectures—beans and sesame paste tucked into cheap white rolls—but he had no idea if its disappearance was a product of the new era or predated it. The first thing that struck him was that the outer walls were gone. Without them it was less a campus than a little town, and the few students braving the stormy weather looked just like regular pedestrians passing down streets made pleasant by the trees that in his day had been few and far between. The bare branches gave scant protection against the wind and rain.

Signs that once hung over imposing doorways now sat alongside them at eye level—Arabic, English, plus a script that could have been Korean.

He took the halting steps of a traveler returning to the world of their childhood, as he tried to remember the way to the administration block. Sally stopped a pair of students, the first girl dark and long-haired, the second a muhajaba with Asian features. When she asked them the way, they answered in English. Sally turned right and made for what looked like a pharaonic temple. He followed. He couldn't remember this building having been here back when he was a student.

A red-headed woman was sitting behind a glass pane with a long, narrow slot in it; the presence of the security barrier seemed at odds with the absence of the outer walls. She gave them a questioning look and Warif read out the appointment number he'd been sent by email. A curt nod and she pressed a button. A device beside her gave a low whine and printed out his degree certificate on a sheet of glossy paper. As they walked away, Warif thought about how the woman hadn't spoken a word. Sally, meanwhile, was laughing at the old ID photo at the top of the document, the downy upper lip and dazed expression.

An hour later, walking though the undersea glass tunnel, that dazed expression was back. It felt as though the surrounding sea might slam in on them at any moment. The eyes of the submerged statues watched blankly, Greek faces on Egyptian torsos. He was hurrying slightly, and Sally sensed his distress. She said that she'd like to get home, too. In the car on the road back to Cairo he fell asleep several times and saw himself swimming among the sunken statues. The water was green.

The water's presence was less imposing the next day. The sky spat flecks that were neither rain nor drizzle and the dirt road through the tombs was empty, almost as if people had given up dying: there were no noisy convoys or wailing caravans, no cars with tinted windows pulled over at random by the roadside or barefoot children begging. There were no strays, even: Warif hadn't seen a single dog or cat, let alone one of those more unexpected animals that occasionally found their way here, wandering from ungated gardens and yards nearby into the silence of the lanes.

At the top of the alley, Wagdi stopped to light a cigarette, leaving Warif to go on alone over the damp earth. Pure chance had spared the family tomb from the government clearances and relocations. It was sandwiched between a pair of Mameluke mausoleums, and the debate over whether or not to move these historical monuments had dragged on long enough that the sudden changes in the country removed the issue from contention. So, they'd remained untouched, and with them the family tomb, whose inhabitants had migrated here over a century ago from Aleppo, their family tree thinning through the generations until nothing remained of the name except Warif's parents, then Warif himself. At least, here in Cairo: there were cousins on his father's side who'd emigrated to South America and had been heard of no more. Warif sometimes wondered if any of them might have returned at some point, if he might have walked past them on these new streets. But the tomb itself had only been reopened once in the past forty years, during his penultimate year in prison, when his journey into madness was forcibly cut short and he was brought back—at half of his original weight—to begin the laborious process of remembering who he was.

As it swung back, the gate mewled like a famished cat, and Warif imagined the rusted iron crumbling and flaking as he scraped it over the dirt. To his left was a towering fig tree that threw shade over the tomb's modest plot. There was precious little sun these days, but the fig's canopy kept the ground dry. He thought of the roots curling through his relatives' bones, and he shuddered. Tucked away behind the open gate on his right was the women's chamber, and next to that, facing the tree, that of the men, where his father and his father's father lay buried side by side. His mother, of course, was with the other women. Together but apart, like at some village celebration, they continued to uphold the millennia-old traditions. It was they who pulled him from his prison madness, the same way they used to wake him when he slept in as a teenager. "If we didn't do it, you'd never wake up at all," his father would growl at him when he got home from Friday prayers, which frequently made his mother angry—"Don't say that, for God's sake!"—the sound of their squabbling weaving into the clamor and smells of Old Cairo, the background hiss of neighbors' TVs, the cooking in the courtyards, the cries of vendors outside, and the blare of strong sunlight that managed to slip in no matter how closely one shuttered the windows and plugged the gaps in the boards across the panes.

A week after his release he knocked on his neighbors' doors to thank them. They were his parents' neighbors, to be honest, even though he'd lived alongside them himself until he graduated. They were the ones who'd accompanied his parents to the tomb and taken care of the burial—with Wagdi's assistance, of course. Actually, it was more that they had helped Wagdi. And though a recently released prisoner might seem to others trapped in time—frozen in the world that predated his incarceration and still talking about things that everybody else has forgotten—what he encounters in them is a stark compression of time's more measured transformations. The suddenly fat or thin, the newly aged and infirm, teeth gone missing, mental powers waning, changes of heart—even beauty and ugliness appear in a new light: the prisoner summons a memory and is left peering at its shards, the shattered remains left by time's passage in the faces that, to his astonishment, still bear the names he knows. And they stare back at him, trying in turn to conjure recognition, their suspicions sharpened by reproach.

It was Wagdi who suggested, very cautiously, that his panic attacks might be a kind of punishment directed inward, a symptom of self-blame. "The rational mind isn't rational, if that makes sense…" he had said during one of his more philosophical moods, going on to add that guilt was the most arbitrary of feelings: a gun cocked and fired blind that wounds our innocence but leaves our true crimes unscathed.

Like coming to after years in a coma, it took Warif time to understand where he was, and who, and just what was going on. It was due to Wagdi's considerable efforts and, at a remove, those of Sally—and because things were already starting to change, too—that he nearly made it to his parents' funeral. He was in the cell, locked in a heated debate with a grocer, an elderly man now dead. As a boy his mother would send him to this grocer to get cheese and honey, and it upset Warif that this man was here when he should be dead—in the sense that it upset many of his convictions about life after death or the lack of it; not that he could say so in front of this man, a pious fellow his father's age. He was in the middle of an argument, then, when suddenly he heard the call for the afternoon prayer. The grocer struggled to his feet, just as he used to in the shop when he was alive. Warif was half-afraid of an invitation to accompany him to the mosque, and wondered, startled, if it was true that we pray after death. Then he heard a familiar voice, sounding as if from the bottom of a well:

"Get up, Warif. Your father is dead."

The door opened and two figures appeared, a pair of silhouettes so tall it was as though they stretched from the ground to the sky. A shard of distant memory drifted down and struck the seafloor of his mind: bedtime stories in which ghosts the size of giraffes, their stiff stick legs like circus stilts, waylaid lost travelers on deserted roads at night. The silhouettes escorted him to a van with a back like a box. He was trying and failing to remember his father's name—he wanted them to call him by his proper name—but then he thought that this must all be a hallucination, and he peered around the box to see if the dead grocer was back from his prayers. There was no one else there. In the van's roof, he saw a small opening that from time to time was blocked out by branches and leaves. Bright sunshine, suddenly quenched by the trees' cover, then sunshine again. A little bird perched on the lip of the opening. When he moved, the bird spotted him and flew away. He looked down at himself. He couldn't see his body. The clothes he wore were huge and his body was somewhere inside them, stumbling around as though in a maze.

Then there were no more branches at the opening, then the sun went out, and he couldn't tell whether the box was still moving or if it had stopped. Distantly, he heard voices—a low growling that would gather and rise then soften and almost disappear—and after a while he started to believe that he had never left the cell at all, and that the two looming shadows, the box where he sat, the branches, the bird, and the growling were all just fragments of dreams. But then the opening reappeared, filled with dawn light, and the box started to move again.

For the first time in years he felt hunger gnawing at him. It troubled him: not the sensation of hunger itself, but feeling it at all. He waited for the bird to come back: when it came, he decided, he would ask it things, anything that came to mind, but now the voice that had told him of his father's death was addressing him, calling to him from the other side of the steel plating:

"Warif! There is no strength save in God! Your mother has joined your father in the House of Truth."

He remembered her name immediately, but there was no shock. Naela. Naela was dead and there was no need any more to go to her, to join her in mourning his father: she had gone to him.

They brought him back to the prison, and as he passed beneath the thick tangle of branches and leaves he heard a siren sounding, a great blaring, and then a light pattering, like a particulate rain against the outside of the box. In the cell, everything was yellow. The floor was a carpet of milled wheat, and he stretched out over it. The grocer was not yet back from his prayers and the yellow was pouring in through the two vents in the door, piling higher and higher, and he thought that he must have followed his parents and that they were burying him, too.

That evening Wagdi had been checking on Warif's parents, one of those infrequent visits he struggled to fit in between work and his home life, all the more difficult since the arrival of his children. He could see how rapidly the diabetes was spreading through Warif's father's body, the arteries constricting practically before his eyes, and how the hand of fate was steadily ratcheting its grip on the mother's heart, a little tighter with every visit. They were increasingly immobile, and he would help them with their more urgent tasks. Increasingly, the father didn't even realize it was him and would call him Warif. He also had to studiously ignore the strange glances of reproach sent his way by the mother. Wagdi hoped that if she ever articulated the feelings behind these looks he'd be able to understand her reasons, but she never did.

She twice reminded her husband to take his medicine that evening. The first time he'd just shaken his head; the second, he muttered that he would, then turned back to the meal he was sharing with Wagdi. They were sitting at the dining table pushed against the wall. A full fifty percent of its surface was covered with boxes of pills and ampules of insulin, the rest with their plates. Beef head and lentil soup: a meal he refused to give up despite his illness, and whose ills he balanced with a strict pill-taking schedule. Had he simply forgotten, then? Had his frayed memory finally fallen apart? Or was it just that he'd made up his mind to ignore his obligation? Whatever the case, his wife stood weeping with her neighbors at dawn the next day, reliving over and over again the story of his last moments—first just to them, then, once he'd come back, to both them and Wagdi. How he'd told her that he could feel his soul lifting out of him *here*, and had pointed to a spot in the middle of his chest. She was gripping the pill bottle and saying, anger in her voice, that he hadn't taken his pills, and Wagdi was unable to hold her gaze, unwilling to meet the mounting reproach in her eyes. She had no idea that she would die just two days later, that after the two exhausting days of the burial, followed by the wake at the Abu Bakr al-Sadiq event hall, she would find herself back at home, screaming in pain and surrounded by black-clad women; that she would clutch at her breast (or her head...accounts differed) then lose consciousness; that when the ambulance finally arrived the medics would pronounce her dead. But that morning she was still alive, alive and angry, and Wagdi believed that she remained angry until she passed away. He also remembered that she hadn't mentioned Warif's name once in all that time, not to say she missed him or that she blamed him, not even to use his name in one of those stock phrases—"Your father's dead, Warif"—that serve as devices to summon the absent into the circle of those present, to join the living with the dead.

In reality—even as Wagdi was attempting (and somewhat succeeding, thanks to connections from his job and the cooperation of Sally, whom he'd been forced to turn to, for all that it weighed heavy on his heart) to secure for Warif an exceptional pass so that he could join his mother in burying his father, and whenever he had a moment to pause and draw breath—what most preoccupied him was something else entirely. It was his memory of the father's last night, his appetite for his final, rich meal, which he ate in the living room without Warif, whose absence of many years was so established that it might as well have been forever, as though this was the natural order of things: that the father should sit and eat with his son's best friend, while the mother looked on and the television buzzed away in the background. Wagdi couldn't get it out of his head: for the first time he'd witnessed death as an act, a choice easily avoided.

All his life—not that he'd ever thought about it too deeply—he'd seen death as inevitable. It was fate, destined to happen however faint the clues that led there, however winding the road or absurd the coincidences that held the plot together, however peculiar even: balconies that collapsed onto the heads of passersby, apricot pits lodging in throats, heart attacks brought on by a last-minute goal in a cup final. But observing the *way* it happened here, he couldn't ignore the fact that if Warif's father had stopped eating with half his meal done, if he'd left the lentil soup untouched, say, or taken his medicine as usual, then he would have been alive the next morning and the morning after that, and maybe even today, and not below the ground with his son standing over him in the Shahin family tomb. In the mother's case, however, her suppressed rage, the loneliness that awaited her with both son and husband gone, were the circumstances (Wagdi wouldn't go so far as to say *causes*) that led to her passing—however burdensome it might be to him (the "professor" as the neighbors called him when they came around to tell him the news just as he had returned home at last, exhausted—in fact, almost dead himself—following the father's wake and his efforts to obtain Warif's pass) to find himself standing once more in the same event hall to receive condolences in place of her son, his friend.

Attendance was scarce, especially in the men's section. He had posted himself at the entrance, then stepped inside to escape the sand. The wind was blowing it through the streets till everything was yellow and existence was reduced to the taste of dust in the throat. The leaves flapped on the trees, which had been gradually growing in number on the other side of the Magra al-Uyoun aqueduct and spreading toward Downtown, like a second wall that separated Wagdi and his world from the neighborhoods whose streets were filling with foreigners and that, as far as he could tell in the course of fleeting visits, were rapidly changing, taking on the image of the newcomers. He had yet to hear what they called the new forest in Tahrir. It was an actual forest, they said, but tamed: a playground for squirrels where bulbuls hopped between branches in sight of the Nile. But he had seen the gazelle in al-Azhar Park with his own eyes, after they pulled the walls down and rolled lawns over the tombs. The speed with which it all happened was astonishing. A new country practically overnight, after three years of gradually increasing tourist numbers and the success of the economic substitution plan, which had granted the people permanent relief from the backbreaking toil that had been their lot for millennia: a monthly stipend funded from the new surplus.

The sudden improvement in the quality of those institutions that received this foreign expertise was the catalyst that set in motion a geometric progression of change, more aid leading to more institutions, supported by the labor of what were known as "middle-ground" nationalities: mostly citizens from Eastern Europe or the former Soviet bloc, with above-average skills and rocky economies back home. It proved more difficult to attract people from Western Europe and the United States. At least at first.

Not that the changes went completely unchallenged. Especially in the early phases there was discontent, but a wave of unpredictable accidents, and their material and human cost, quickly convinced any holdouts of the plan's advantages. These accidents were sometimes comical, such as the time the pants of the Cairo orchestra split in synch as they sat to begin the inaugural concert of the New Opera House; or tragic, as in the case of the bullet train disaster, when it struck the roof of a tunnel running under a fisherman's village on the north coast and carried off the entire settlement on top of the front cars for a final, five-kilometer journey at half the speed of sound before depositing it all—houses and shops and animals, plus the village school—into the sea. Whether they provoked sarcasm or grief, they lent a visceral impetus to the *Foreigners are our oil* campaign, which argued that the country should compensate for its scarcity of natural resources by recruiting overseas talent in ever-greater numbers. Think of the advantages: an excellent education married to a pragmatic mindset and then, thanks to their passports, no cause to fear transgressions by the local authorities. The dream, or so some dared to dream it, was that a foreigner-run authority would be swapped in to replace every single local incompetent authority (which is to say, nearly all of them) until the country regained its footing. Inflation, in this new reckoning, meant only an increase of one party (that is to say, local or foreign) at the expense of the other.

Though he'd lived through it all himself, had witnessed it and been a part of it—indeed had benefitted from it like everyone else through a fixed monthly stipend that the state added to the salary he got (because the state still regarded his work as vital)—Wagdi still didn't have a clear, chronological understanding of events as they had happened. He only realized this as he was explaining things to Warif, after his friend had gotten out of prison. Even as he spoke, he would find himself re-remembering events, even his place within them, and begin to doubt that something had happened as he thought or had the effect he imagined. Only naturally, he retained a degree of skepticism about Warif's claims regarding the curious resemblance between the country's transformation and the post he'd published and, so he insisted, for which he had been detained one breeze-washed evening on Adly Street.

This was one of the two primary tasks that Wagdi had worried about—that had worried at him—in the months following Warif's release from prison and his return to the apartment in Old Cairo. Two interconnected tasks: the first was his duty to explain the changes to his friend; the second was his role in shaping events both now and to come, by preparing those future news reports. But he also had to attempt to persuade Warif that his father's death, then his mother's, were weightless events: purely random and in no way ominous.

He had to be careful, beyond even his customary caution, as he communicated to his friend—bewildered and subject to panic attacks—that what had killed his father was an appetite for beef head and not the unjust and arbitrary incarceration of his son. He also realized, as he explained to Warif the new situation in the country, that his friend—who still held tight to his claim that his Facebook post had been the source of his misfortune, whether that post had been the impetus for the changes imposed on the country or whether the similarities were pure coincidence—had managed to convince himself over the course of those long years behind bars that he had been in the wrong. Maybe he hadn't deserved to be punished so severely, but the fact remained that what he'd written was wrong, especially when the country was going through such difficult times. Whether voluntarily or not, this was how his mind chose to arrange things: he had done wrong, had paid the price for doing wrong, and as a consequence his parents died from grief. His subsequent feelings of guilt (rational or otherwise) led to his panic attacks.

Which is why Wagdi ended up bringing him here, to visit their graves, because avoiding it—avoiding the visit, covering up the truth, and running away from memory—would never work: it would break out in the form of nightmares, in terrors. Carefully, artfully, concealing his own sense of hopelessness invoked by the avoidable death he himself had been unfortunate enough to witness, Wagdi began to drip-feed Warif the idea that it had been a normal death, quite free of wider significance; one that, let us say, was bound to have happened sooner or later, which had spared him the need to bear witness. In other words, then, the guilt and panic attacks Warif felt were not a karmic consequence of Warif's responsibility for their deaths, but rather a punishment he meted out to himself for what he had done to himself. That was to say—and here Wagdi grew warier still—for putting himself in danger and thus squandering years of his life. It was this self-pity that was the true source of his feelings; the panic attacks were simply attacks on himself—shots fired by a blind gunman.

Maybe this explained why Warif now found himself standing on the dirt floor of the men's burial chamber in the family tomb, filled—if the expression serves—with emptiness. The woman's chamber was double locked with an additional bike chain. The room was roofed, but he could smell rain in the dirt beneath his feet. Once more, he thought of the fig's roots branching through bones, and rainwater running down them to make little lakes in which the dead were swimming. He saw his father floating on his back, just as he used to do on those fleeting holidays at the company's summer resort in Agami, while his mother sat on the sand counting how many sandwiches were left, and he between them, neither out at sea nor quite ashore, wading in the brief stretch where wet encounters dry, the low waves running in over his feet and knees then exposing both as they fell back. Nothing. Wagdi was right. It was like standing at a stranger's grave, like he was attending the funeral of a friend's distant uncle just to keep him company. He wondered if his attempts to go mad in Cell 61 (the number, suddenly, came back to him) had succeeded, if he'd actually managed to pop a few of those brain cells. He would prefer to believe that this was the reason for these unanticipated emotional blanks.

A shadow fell at his feet: Wagdi, here to hurry him along. They left what was left of the City of the Dead, and as they passed through the gate, Warif thought he caught sight of some newcomers stepping soft-footed into one of the Mameluke mausoleums.

They sat side by side in silence as the Lanus headed out of the city toward the new neighborhoods. The residential zone was surrounded on all sides by desert and half-built buildings, but inside the streets were crowded. Warif spotted a phalanx of office workers praying on green matting down a side alley.

In a vast open-plan space crammed with workstations and computers, Wagdi had a corner office, set slightly apart from the rest, from where he had a clear view over the main hall. Warif sat and watched him work. With February nearly at an end, he was drafting reports for March, and from time to time would read one out loud. Warif couldn't tell if Wagdi wanted his opinion or was simply trying to entertain him. There was a piece about Ramadan lanterns: a company had printed a famous actor's face on their lanterns without obtaining permission and the actor wasn't just demanding compensation but that every single one of the company's lanterns be taken down from shopfronts and cafés, from all the streets and alleys where they hung. Warif liked it. He remembered Wagdi telling him the rumors about Umm Kulthoum's restored villa in Zamalek. Those rumors were no less "realistic" than the news it was his friend's job to invent. Why didn't the team make a report out of them, he asked? About the claims of those who, passing by, had said they'd heard voices raised in conversation, the sounds of partying and music, or had seen distinguished gentlemen in tarbooshes stepping through the villa's gates at dawn. It was, in Warif's opinion anyway, a quite enchanting rumor, and an innocent one. Timeless, in fact. The report needn't state it as fact, either: it should simply say that there were stories going around. It might even be a good thing: it would keep people entertained. Even better, it might promote tourism in the neighborhood.

"You and tourism! You're beyond help..." Wagdi laughed. He paused, then added, "I mean, we need foreign tourists, not senile music lovers."

When Warif didn't smile, Wagdi reached over to touch his knee in apology. But then he broke into laughter, so loud that a few of those typing away in the hall glanced up before ducking back to their screens.

The next day, walking through old Maadi, he wondered whether Wagdi might actually use his idea. Here at last was a neighborhood untouched by change, perhaps because it had always been a place for foreigners. He had no trouble finding the café. Sally was already there, sitting with her friends. He didn't know anyone. He sat next to a petite woman with features he found difficult to decipher, but he understood why when she told him she was from Kazakhstan. She was named Jalnoor. Facing him was a middle-aged man, powerfully built and pleasant seeming. Sally introduced him as Jakob, from Poland. A skinny woman about the same height as Sally was named Sara. European-Egyptian like herself.

A couple of quickly downed drinks later, as they were eating a light supper, Sally casually gestured toward Jakob and said, as though she were saying nothing at all, "Oh yeah, Jakob's the guy who got your job."

10

FLYING RATS

Sally didn't agree with Warif that Maadi hadn't changed. At a volume amplified by many glasses of wine, she said, "You don't have eyes in your head."

Not that Warif was able to hear her clearly anyhow. The chatter and din in the restaurant ran together into a white noise that hissed in his ears. He just managed to catch something about there being bars everywhere in Maadi now; that despite its old reputation as a neighborhood full of foreigners, there had been almost nowhere that served alcohol. Egyptian bullshit had put its stamp on the place. But that, Sally was saying, wasn't the only change. The air, the atmosphere, the attitude—there was a new lightness that had been missing before, despite its expat aura, despite the trees and villas, the pampered dogs and roller skaters.

Jakob was trying his best to engage him in conversation, but Warif kept his responses clipped, barely audible. He looked past Jakob, eyes scanning. There was some half-hearted chat with the girl from Kazakhstan, too. He was a getting a clearer look at her now; a history of tribal lineages, Turks and Tartars, warred and married in her face. Her eyes held something powerful, intelligence and no little life experience. By now, he could tell that she wasn't as young as her small frame had first suggested: his age, perhaps, even a little older. She was complaining, laughing, about the pigeons that flocked in the little square outside her house nearby.

"But isn't that a nice thing?"

He was trying to get her to talk, to avoid meeting Jakob's gaze.

"No!" she said loudly. "I hate pigeons. They're flying rats."

And with an ambiguous gesture that could have meant everybody or nobody at all, she went on, "I can't believe you eat them here."

"Well, not everybody eats horses either," Warif heard himself say. "You know, like where you come from."

The Kazakh stared at him for a moment, startled, then turned to Sally and said, grinning ear to ear, "So! Your friend's not so simple!"

"He knows a few things," Sally said, smiling.

He heard Jakob say, with a sort of forced intimacy, "I'd really like it if we could talk about the job, Warif. I've no doubt I could learn from your experience."

"He wants his old job back," Sally said in a tone that Warif couldn't quite interpret.

"Why?" asked Jakob. He sounded surprised. "I envy you… I wish I could get a salary for doing nothing. That's the dream, isn't it?"

"He could find other work if he wanted…"

"If you like hard work, I suppose…"

"Is it true you were in prison?"

This last question was from Jalnoor, the Kazakh pigeon-hater. Everyone stared at her. She became defensive. "What? That's what Sally told us!"

Then Jakob, amicable as ever, said,

"Well he's not there now."

"Sure," said Jalnoor, "but what if he left something there? People who leave things in places tend to go back to get them."

She grinned as she said this, then looked straight at Warif. "Not even a smile?"

"Don't be upset with her," murmured Jakob. "Her country's a prison, too."

Jalnoor glanced around, mock-nervously. "Keep your voice down," she said, "and leave my country alone."

At last, Warif had found his voice:

"I'm not upset," he said. "Anyway, it's all a question of what *kind* of thing I might have left there. It doesn't have to be a physical object."

"Ah!" said Jalnoor, and gave him a playful slap on the hand. "Stop philosophizing!"

This was the lightness that Sally had mentioned just moments before. It was starting to sweep him away. Not for the first time, but this time under the influence of wine and screwdrivers, he felt as though the years gone by had never been. He didn't fight the feeling. He told himself that his life before, the student days and the job, simply hadn't mattered; even his aborted attempts to translate novels and write short stories of his own had only ever received genuine support from Wagdi, and then only out of Wagdi's affection for him, not from any critical engagement. The seven years of prison were seven blanks to be added to the thirty that had gone before, and given all that, how fortunate he was to be here, now, sitting with these people in a Maadi that, according to Sally, had changed more than he could imagine. Even more fortunate, if Jakob was to be believed, that he didn't have to work. He was thinking about what Jalnoor had said, whether he had indeed left anything behind in prison, and also noticing how remarkably similar Sara and Sally looked. They could have been sisters, he thought, and wondered if Sara, like Sally, had a predilection for cruelty.

SLEEP PHASE

He propped his elbow on the table, rested his chin on his palm, and turned his head to the side as he thought, his thoughts given wings by the wine, that it wasn't simply that time was relative, but that time was relativity itself. If a few instants of suffering could erase a lifetime of happiness (supposing there was such a thing), then so too could a few minutes of lightheartedness, such as he felt, fleetingly, in this here and now, convert years of despair into nothing but a distant memory, to be recalled with a wry joke or grin. Luckily for him, he thought, a man didn't need to balance out years of one thing with years of the other before he could crack a smile—and then he smiled despite himself, because Jalnoor had reached out two fingers and pretended to smooth his eyebrows straight.

"Don't scowl," she said. "Don't be upset. You can philosophize if that's what makes you happy."

He smiled because she was acting like she really seemed to believe that's what was going on in his mind: philosophizing.

He stood up and almost lost his balance. For a few seconds he stayed perfectly still, then, though no one had asked, he announced that he was going to the bathroom. He set off without the slightest idea where he was going, only to find himself by the café's glass door. So he went outside. There were a number of long tables laid out in the square, most of them occupied. The low laughter and conversation were scarcely louder than the background music washing from some hidden speaker. There was a nip in the air, though with the booze warming him he couldn't ready tell how cold it was. On one side of the square he saw a heater and a number of pigeons clustering around it for warmth. He thought of calling Jalnoor, then he realized that his phone was vibrating in his pocket and the ringtone was getting louder. The number he didn't recognize, and he didn't get many calls in any case: Wagdi mostly, Sally occasionally, text messages for appointments with the unplaceable men and translucent women. He answered. A familiar voice said, "It's Souad. Have you heard from Wagdi? He hasn't been home since yesterday."

He felt his blood drain away. Several seconds passed until the adrenaline began to spike through the surface of his stupor.

"No," he said at last.

From the way she spoke it was like she didn't believe him, or hoped he was lying. "So what do I do now?"

As if she were depositing the problem in his lap. Who else's?

"Maybe he went back to the village?"

Even as he said it he felt like a fool, and then had to listen to the inevitable rejoinder: Wagdi wouldn't have left without letting her know.

"Plus, I called his family and they don't know anything."

Warif's knee started trembling, the way it had all those years ago on Adly Street, but he tried to calm her down as best he could. His voice barely shook:

"I'll take care of it."

He hung up. There were even more pigeons around the heater; the laughter and the music were unchanged. Turning back to the glass door, he could see Sally and her friends at the corner table. Sara was saying something and they all seemed to be hanging on her words. Something brushed his shoulder and he stiffened: a woman had tapped his shoulder, wanting to go in. As he stepped aside to let her pass, he was already telling himself that the crisis was over. It was an old technique of his, which he deployed in times of trouble. He would try and picture the day after the crisis: the first day of health following an illness, the first days of the holidays after the exams. He used to believe that when his father died he would use the same method: he would spend the night vigil beside the corpse visualizing the third day when the wake was done and the burial over and he could go home to sleep. That's what he'd believed as he began his prison sentence, and what he continued to believe as the weeks, then months, then years dragged on, until he gave up entirely and tried taking that irrevocable leap into madness. But he'd never once pictured his mother dying, neither before prison nor in the cell. And now? Now what? What was he saying? Wagdi! Should he try and concentrate on the day after his friend was found, on the day they'd sit on the balcony together again? But it wasn't a matter of waiting. He must search.

11

GAZELLES

Two of everything: hospitals, shelters, police stations, traffic systems and censorships, bureaus of investigation and surveillance. It never occurred to him that he'd have to go hunting through two parallel systems, the original version and the newcomers' knockoff, through the old streets that had changed so radically and the new streets built to mimic the old.

The furthest he'd gotten, with the assistance of Sally and the organization where Wagdi worked, was a recording from a surveillance camera. It showed Wagdi's Lanus, just before dawn, traveling down a highway that divided a new neighborhood from a local district. Wagdi's regular route home from work. The car slowed, then suddenly swerved and pulled over. Wagdi stepped out and began to walk off, but then he paused as if he'd seen something—though nothing could be seen in the footage. He moved toward what he saw, somewhere in the deep shadow beneath the trees that lined a sidewalk and stopped again, this time as though speaking to someone. Then he stepped up onto the sidewalk and disappeared beneath the canopy of a tree. He hadn't been seen again.

A tow truck had deposited the Lanus back at the apartment, on the pavement with its scattering of café chairs and the cats coiling around the kebab stand, beneath the looming tower blocks that divvied up the narrow lanes. Souad was sitting in the salon, the kids out of sight, scolding them every time they ventured out of the bedroom. She still had the presence of mind to offer Warif a cup of tea that remained untouched.

He couldn't have just evaporated into thin air, she said. We're bound to find him, was Warif's reply. And then, simultaneously and out loud, they asked the same question: Had Wagdi upset anyone? Both knew that it wasn't in his nature to anger a soul; he had never so much as teased an animal as a boy, never caused trouble in class or upset his teachers, never gotten on the wrong side of his superiors at work.

The voice of the muezzin calling the sunset prayer, a rapid recitation from the corner below the building, sounded through the salon and was followed by silence. Warif asked if the kids were still going to school, but when Souad answered, he suddenly couldn't understand her, as though she was speaking a language he'd never heard before. Then the wall behind her, the dark red expanse above the sofa's backrest, started pulsing rhythmically. He heard Souad asking him a worried voice, "Are you all right?"

What followed was a series of clipped impressions, strung like a surrealist montage. It began with a cup of cold water in which two spoonfuls of sugar slowly dissolved, then moved to the boy's bed in the children's room, where he lay sprawled with his feet hanging over the end. As his eyes were closing, he thought he heard a train whistle in the distance. Then he was getting up every few seconds, though perhaps it was minutes or even longer. He shouldn't be here, he felt. Next he was beating Wagdi at backgammon. They had the board out on his desk at work. The desk was empty except for the game, and Warif's father was there, watching intently, waiting to play the winner. Then all three of them were back at the apartment on Adly Street. His mother had made them a platter of grilled fish and the aroma filled the apartment. The number of rooms in the apartment had multiplied and all the windows were thrown open, and with his parents looking on, Sally asked if he'd finally decided on a date for their wedding. It surprised him, because hadn't they agreed to wait till his mother got better? But all the same he obliged: a day in early summer. Then something warm touched his neck. He gave a jerk of his head, but the touches kept coming and he opened his eyes.

Light from the hall was filtering into the children's bedroom and he could see Zeinab peering at him. She was tapping her finger against his neck and smiling. Souad called to her to get out of the room, and the little girl backed toward the door. Then she stopped. Why was the back of his neck all those different colors, she wanted to know? Unconsciously, he reached back and caressed his nape. He didn't know what to say. Then Souad called again and Zeinab was gone.

Warif levered himself upright, knocked gently on the half-open door, then, a little shamefaced, shuffled out of the room and straight into the bathroom across the corridor.

With the assistance of the glow from his phone's screen and the bathroom mirror he inspected the dark lines that striped the width of his white neck like bruises from a noose. A sign that the insulin was starting to kick in, and he thought how in the end he would inherit the disease that had killed his father. But he also knew himself, that it wouldn't bother him yet, not now in the beginning, and that he'd use the pain's onset to his advantage, that he'd accustom himself to the change and leave the real suffering for later. Another knock, this time on the inside of the bathroom door, and he came out into the salon. Souad asked him how he was feeling. In her face he saw, or thought he saw, a blend of weariness, shame, and disappointment. But she still managed to inquire if he'd eaten anything, and though he hadn't, not a thing all day, he told her that he had. A little soup, at least, she insisted. The soup was warm and comforting and the children, now given a freer rein, started to play beside him as he ate. Souad brought him another cup of tea. He felt the tears brimming in his eyes and got to his feet, though at the same time he knew he didn't ever want to leave.

As he left the building he had the impression that he was being watched: disquieting stares. He tried to act casual as he looked for a taxi to carry him out of the neighborhood.

The next day he was pulling up to the trees beneath which Wagdi had disappeared, on the edge of the blind spot between the CCTV coverage from the Dutch Teaching Institute on the right side of the highway and the pole-mounted security camera in the vacant plot to the left. He got out of the taxi and crossed the road, weaving between cars that hurtled at top speed toward the entrance of a tunnel.

There was a sort of open space beneath the trees, but there was nobody there that he could see. He walked along the high wall behind them. The wall kinked left and he followed it.

The wall began to get lower and the ground rose to meet it. Just beyond where the road ran into the tunnel there was a large expanse of open ground and facing it, to Warif's left, a line of bulldozers and construction vehicles, huge and empty. They must be about to build some more of those replica neighborhoods, thought Warif: vast tower blocks of miniscule apartments, narrow lanes and crowded markets, minarets and microbuses. Right now, though, it was the silence that dominated, that and emptiness. As he walked he tried to imagine what had prompted Wagdi to get out of his car here, in this wasteland; he remembered Wagdi's fear of dogs and thought to himself that if Wagdi had owned a dog then he could have brought it here to pick up the scent.

The sun would dim, recover its strength, then dim again, slipping back behind the scudding clouds. Warif looked up and saw…what? Great birds wheeling far overhead. Eagles? The rising ground leveled off then began to fall away and he was able to recover his breath. To his right, the wasteland began to show patches of green; the sight of it was somehow clean, calming, and also out of place, like a cool night breeze that takes a wrong turn into noonday heat. Then the green thickened and spread, the grass grew longer, and scattered trees appeared in the distance. This must be, or at least could be, one of the extensions that linked up with al-Azhar Park. In which case, he reasoned, he was currently walking where tombs and mausoleums once stood. Over graves. It was slightly frightening. Something furry scampered through the brush in front of him. A rat? he thought. A particularly big rat… He paused for a moment, then continued forward, more tentatively now. The scent of grass filled his nose.

Then he saw the creature move again. And again. It was a hare. Could it be the same hare that had stared at him the day he'd first come to the park? But this one didn't so much as glance at him, slipping away through the long grass. Nor for that matter were there any visitors lying on these lawns, no stands of cypress, elm, and cherry. In fact, the ground here was hardly lawn at all: all slopes and dips, runnels that led him left and right but always downward until at last the green around him started to rise again in walls that sloped up to a kind of hill country. The grass was rougher now, untended, and from everywhere came the calls of strange birds, weaving in and out of the music that the wind made as it passed between the interlocking hilltops. Despite the dry weather, he felt the ground becoming damp and it sloped ever more steeply down until he was forced to lean back to keep his balance. He followed the incline down and to the right, until he found himself facing a spring.

He approached the pond with a kind of wonder. The water was clear, almost transparent, and its surface held a sky full of scudding clouds. He bent forward till he saw his face, then turned his head right and left, watching the movement mirrored in the water as though checking that the reflection was really him. On the far side of the lake, the water let out into a confusion of poplar and bay, their trunks tangled into a little wood. But perhaps not so little as it appeared, because its size was hidden by the slopes of more hills and the green dips between them.

Something lightly touched his right leg and he glanced down. A little gazelle. It lifted its face to him and its eyes seemed as green-gold as the ones that Sally had told him about. But everything here was green, he thought to himself. The sunlight passing through the clouds, the shade cast by the trees and embraced by the grass, the empty shoreline of this enchanted pond.

The gazelle brushed his leg again then stepped forward and paused, looking back at him as though it wanted him to follow. He took two paces toward it and it set off running, darting around a low rise. As he rounded the corner after it, he saw a long sunken path running into the distance, like a streambed shaded by willows and more poplar and bay. It wasn't the sight of the trees that held Warif motionless, though, but the gazelles. At first he saw just one, the twin of the one he'd followed, but then he noticed another, and then, as his eyes adjusted to the sheer density of color, the greens of the leaves and grass and the browns and grays of the trunks, he realized that nearly all the movement he could see wasn't branches and their foliage, but rather a seemingly unending number of small gazelles, tan and green, yellow, black and white, all staring his way as if in shock. Then they gave their call. *Salil*, he thought, remembering Sally's description. A harsh croak, a strained intake of breath. Then they all bolted simultaneously, scattering before his eyes like a puzzle fracturing, and bouncing away down the tree-lined path.

Warif followed them. To be precise, he followed in their general direction, because in no time they had disappeared, melting into the dense green. He walked down the sunken path that was like a streambed, or the streambed that resembled a path roofed with branches and birds whose bodies he could not see but whose song never ceased. He couldn't make out where the path ended; it appeared instead to divide and branch into other, similar paths, each fringed by tree trunks that knotted and fretted together. Later, he would wonder when they were planted, or how they'd been brought here—and also: Where were the people? It was as if he was walking through a pre-human landscape. He glimpsed, sensed rather, the shapes and shadows of creatures skittering around his feet and ducking behind trees, and the calls that sounded from the canopies suggested a great variety of birds. He asked himself if all this great profusion of nature would remain as it was when summer arrived, or whether it had already survived the summers he'd spent in his cell, wanting only madness.

Now he could hear the sound of water bubbling and splashing, as though flowing with force or falling from a height, but he couldn't see where it came from, the same way he was surrounded by birdsong but hadn't seen a single bird. Just ahead, in the wall of a hill's slope, he saw an opening like a cave mouth, and within it, a long tunnel stretching away. It looked endless. He halted, unsure whether to go on. He glanced back at the wood through which he'd walked and now seemed like a vast and boundless forest, then turned to the tunnel. Remember, he told himself sternly, you're not here to go on a stroll, you're here to look for your friend. He took a deep breath and walked in.

For a considerable distance, his way was lit with light from the entrance. The floor was dewy at the start, but at some point turned rocky, though at first he didn't noticed the change. But what he'd feared might happen, that the tunnel would narrow until it became hard to breathe or too tight to press on, never came to pass: the roof didn't slope down toward his unprotected head, and indeed, even though there wasn't the slightest trace of a human presence, it felt as though the whole thing had been constructed for people to use.

At last it grew too dark to see and he switched on his phone's flashlight. The passage was as wide as ever, easily enough for three Warifs to walk abreast, while the ground maintained its scrubby wildness, peppered with thorns and rocky outcrops. The smell was earthy and it never once felt as though the air was running out, though he'd been walking so long that rivulets of sweat ran like snakes down his back and chest. He kept himself going with the thought that the fresh air must mean an exit somewhere up ahead.

Just as he felt the ground start to slope upward, the exit appeared. He had been pushing himself to keep up a steady pace, still worried that at the last moment the ceiling might drop down and force him to crawl, but before it did, at the same moment as he felt a strange kind of calm descending over him (which he would subsequently interpret as the satisfaction of knowing he hadn't abandoned his search for Wagdi without trying as hard as he could), he saw light ahead. He climbed toward it. The opening was filled with sunlight—the swift clouds must all have raced away—but the tunnel was gradually filling with a rank and oppressive stench.

At last he stepped back out into the world, eyes clamped shut against the force of the light, almost vomiting from the smell. He was in a kind of open sandy zone, like a desert. There was the roar of traffic in the distance, though he couldn't see any sign of it. Parked on the sand, surrounding him on all sides, were more construction vehicles, abandoned, sand heaped in drifts against their sides.

He set off in the direction of the traffic. The smell, bad enough already, was getting stronger, and when he walked around a huge spool looped with thick cabling he discovered where it had been coming from. He could barely see, so intense was the reek, but he narrowed his eyes and took in the view. Dozens—no, hundreds—of dead animals: cats and dogs, the occasional donkey or horse, even a few camels. They were lying alone on their sides, or heaped in piles. The ground where they lay tilted downward, as though to a cliff edge, and swarms of flies floated overhead, their buzzing almost loud enough to drown out the noise of the cars.

He staggered away, emptied his stomach, then forced himself to walk back and take another look, to make sure that there were no humans among the multitude. When he was sure, he turned away and pressed on to the hidden highway, walking uphill and away from the mass grave at his back. He climbed and climbed, as though walking to the sky, until he came at last to level ground and asphalt, finally laying his eyes on the cars he'd been hearing the whole time.

He never told anyone about what he had seen, not about the secret spring and the gazelles in the hidden avenue beneath the trees, not about the endless tunnel or the dead animals. He simply explained to Sally, one evening as they were getting ready to go out, that he'd gone searching in the area where Wagdi had last been seen. The authorities must have already looked there, she said. He just shook his head. There was no way they could have seen what he'd seen.

Sally and her friends were going to a concert at the open-air theater at the Ain al-Sira lake. She'd tricked him. Having said, not for the first time, that he mustn't wallow in his misery, she suggested meeting up with some friends, conveniently forgetting to mention the concert. What annoyed him was that when they arrived, Jakob was there too. "He's a good friend of yours, now, is he?" Warif muttered to himself, meaning to ask her outright when they had a moment alone together. Or should he ask whether

Jakob was her lover? He asked after the feisty Kazakh, but apparently she wouldn't be coming. A smiling Sally told him that Jalnoor had work.

He realized he'd never asked Jalnoor what she did. A lawyer, Sally told him, but she had other interests. "Better if Jalnoor tells you herself." For no reason that he could see, Sally laughed as she said this, but before he could ask why, a hush fell over the audience and the concert began: a Vivaldi violin concerto. Warif found himself thinking of Souad and the children in that cramped living room with the narrow balcony overlooking the narrow street, and he tried to force himself back to the present. Had Wagdi ever gone to concerts like this while he'd been in prison? he wondered. The concert lights illuminated the water behind the orchestra and made it feel as though the stage was afloat on its glinting surface, the concerto rising and falling as softly as the wavelets shaped by the breeze at the heart of the lake. And despite the lights, the gently rocking moon's reflection was clearly visible.

He felt fingers lightly shake him and he opened his eyes. It was over. They were all looking at him, smiling. It must seem like he'd been asleep the whole time, he thought, and the ghost of a memory came to him, of drowsy afternoons in the apartment in Adly Street. Suddenly, he had a very clear recollection of how they used to call it their "sleep phase," and how they'd laugh as they said it. How it was his favorite thing they did together. He never should have gone to buy those cigarettes, he thought.

Then he realized that Jakob was saying something to him. Something about a jump? Did Warif want to come?

It took him a while to realize that they were talking about a parachute jump over the park, and he thought back to the parachutes he'd noticed the day he saw his first gazelle. Then he remembered what the young man had said about parachutes in the big cell with the blue and yellow light, that he'd never tried it himself, but had heard it was easy and safe and fun. Like a train ride. They wouldn't be jumping out of a plane, Sally added. She was going, and so was Jalnoor. Without knowing quite why, Warif heard himself saying that he'd be the first to jump.

He said his goodbyes and was just wandering away from the group when he heard Sally call his name. She came toward him in the moonlight and without any preamble, asked him if he was still having those panic attacks. "I've got something that might help," she said, reaching into her handbag and pulling out a tiny white pill trapped between fingertip and thumb. She brought it up to his lips and when he jerked his head back in alarm, she laughed and said, "Don't be scared, it's only a sedative!"

She gave him a strip and told him to take one a

day. As simple as that? he thought, but said nothing.

He strolled down to the lakeshore. There was no one there except a few young women in summer clothes, pacing slowly between the water's edge and the main road. One was holding the leash of a small, incredibly fluffy white dog, which began bouncing around the bike lane. He walked on, following the road, and soon came to an empty bus stop that was walled with brightly lit advertising screens. On one, a man was kissing a delighted looking woman. The light had attracted spiders and moths alongside other, less readily identifiable insects, most likely from the lake.

A bus pulled up and a pair of women got out. In English, they asked Warif for directions, but the address they gave meant nothing to him and he had to apologize. They smiled at him and walked off. He went the other way, away from the bus stop and the women, the walkers by the lakeshore and the merry dog, and as he walked he was overwhelmed by a powerful yet unfamiliar emotion, a feeling he found hard to explain. The night before last, he'd had a dream. In the dream, he was walking through Heliopolis. The neighborhood had reclaimed its former verdant greenery and well-heeled pedestrians clicked along its sidewalks. There was a woman. She looked just like Sally, with the same green eyes and slim waist, but she was slightly shorter than Sally, and maybe a little older. It was her mother, he realized, walking calmly and contentedly through streets that were just the way she remembered them, and at an age when she would have known them. He approached her and waited for her to recognize him—just as Sally had led him to believe that she would—but his expectant expression was met with just a brief glance, a fleeting smile, and then she walked straight past him. He wondered why they'd let her wander off on her own, and then, immediately following this thought, and almost with a sense of triumph, he understood the congruency of it all—which was to say the appearance of the streets and the age of the woman—was rigged. Simulated, so to speak: another piece of evidence with which to persuade Sally of his theory that the world we thought we lived in was a lie. Then, just as suddenly, and with the clarity that revelation has in dream, he realized that he must be dreaming. Even so, he didn't immediately wake up, but tumbled instead into a chain of other dreams, increasingly disjointed and fragmented, that lasted all night long.

12

A BREAK FROM TWO GODS

As he came to the entrance of his building, he noticed that the cranes and bulldozers had crept closer. For the first time he could remember, the street was silent: not a sound from the apartments; the balconies shuttered, the windows dark. Had people left the building? He'd ask the taciturn doorman what he'd heard.

Another day without any news about Wagdi's disappearance. He hadn't left a website unscrolled or page unturned in the local papers. Wagdi's own organization continued to pump out reports that Wagdi had probably prepared himself weeks before, without offering a single comment on his absence. Better to keep it quiet, they'd told Warif: say nothing until we have all the facts—or any facts. On social media, which he'd started haunting again using minimalist accounts—no personal data or pictures—there was an argument raging on the subject of shoes: Could guests wear them inside a host's house, or did good manners dictate that they take them off at the door? If it wasn't for Souad, her faltering questions on the phone, her seeking him out from time to time to help her invent explanations for the children why their father was still gone, he might almost have believed that his oldest friend had never existed at all. As for Wagdi's family back in the village, not one of its many members, for reasons of their own, regarded the fact he had vanished as at all remarkable.

Jalnoor invited him to a party at the apartment she rented in a hotel complex that overlooked the restored bridge in Boulaq Aboul Ala. There was a dancing pole in her living room. This, then, was one of the "other interests" Sara had been referring to the night of the concert. Jalnoor no longer struck him as petite so much as svelte, a body honed by dance and yoga. She was a generous host as well, constantly pressing drinks and canapes on him.

He chose to sit out on the balcony, watching people stroll along the looping walkway with its ironwork that would occasionally part to let the sails of Nile boats slide through, bracketed by lights and music. On the far bank glowed the island neighborhood of Zamalek. He could see more, and more various, trees there than ever before; it looked like a canvas, pulsing with color. He looked out at the scene, trying to push through the heaviness that had filled his head since he'd started taking the sedatives. They made him want to throw up sometimes, but this was the price he'd chosen to pay.

He heard voices below the building. They had a rhythmic, singsong quality, like a chant, and looking down he saw a group of young men and women, some carrying signs. A woman was walking ahead of the rest, leading the call and response in a language that Warif tried, and failed, to identify. There was a strange mix of determination and levity in their tone. Some of the girls had multicolored handcuffs around their wrists. The dense crowds parted as they proceeded down the street; some bystanders took pictures. Warif tried reading the signs, but the script was no less indecipherable than the chanting. He turned his attention back to the apartment behind him.

Jakob was sitting in the living room close to the balcony door. He was more or less Warif's height, but he had a neatly pointed beard, and his hair fell down to his shoulders. Warif wryly imagined what would have happened if he'd grown his hair out like that back when the job was his. Jakob was drinking steadily but it didn't seem to have affected him at all, and Sally, for reasons best known to herself—perhaps her longstanding loyalty to the god of cruelty—seemed unusually attentive to him. She kept leaning over to whisper in his ear; they'd both laugh, and her green eyes would shine, not with happiness or joy so much as with contentment.

Warif got up to go to the bathroom. At the far end of the corridor, beneath a dim light, he saw Jalnoor and Sara kissing. When they realized he was standing there staring, Sara pointed to the bathroom door and laughed. "It's that way!"

Back in the living room, Sally called him over. "Jakob wants to talk to you about something, but you mustn't get upset."

Lightheaded from the vodka, he answered in Arabic, "Does he want to propose to you?"

An expression of contempt crossed her face.

"I'm not joking," she said in English.

He looked at Jakob, and waved his hand, as if to ask what he wanted. Jakob slid something from his wallet.

"Look, I know that this is a sensitive subject and that you really want your job back. That's none of my business; it's not my decision, after all. But I did do this…"

He held out his hand. It was a plastic card with Warif's picture and a series of numbers.

"I did what I could. Put in a request that your stipend at least be equivalent to the job's current salary. A foreigner's salary, that is."

Warif took it. It was like a standard credit card, embossed with shining golden letters that read *Associate Card*. Except for Wagdi, thought Warif to himself, he didn't have any friends. But Jakob hadn't finished.

"You can use it to open a bank account. I know it's not exactly what you want and I understand that for you this isn't a question of money—well, to be honest, I'm not sure I really *do* understand… Anyway, this is the best I could manage. The thing is, and I'll be honest with you again, given what I know about the changes to the organization over the last few years, I'm fairly certain that your request will be denied."

Jakob stopped and took a breath. Sally's green eyes were fixed on Warif's face with an intensity that reminded him of the old days. Sara and Jalnoor wandered into the room from the corridor but, sensing immediately that something was going on, paused at the door.

"You've had a load of interviews in the last few months," Jakob went on, "or let's say that they've deigned to talk to you. Now, I couldn't say why that is, because no one's ever gotten their old job back before. Maybe those interviews weren't real. I mean, maybe they were for research: a kind of investigation, if you like. That's only my opinion, of course."

"I think you should take it, Warif…" said Sally.

"Honestly, don't worry; I'm not upset," said Warif. "I mean, I assumed it would make me mad, but I'm not. I don't know why."

He staggered as he got to his feet, and for a few seconds he had to stand quite still. He was thinking that he should thank them both, but he knew that any gesture would seem forced; even leaving the party would feel theatrical. All the same, he wanted to go. Jalnoor went with him to the front door and as the elevator doors opened she gave him a quick hug and told him to take care of himself.

A headache was setting in as he arrived home, so he decided to keep on drinking. He hunted for the bottle of scotch that Wagdi had given him, and as he searched he suddenly remembered a conversation they'd had, long ago now, where Wagdi claimed that he took the world too seriously because he wasn't drinking enough. He unscrewed the cap and started to down the whiskey. He felt weightless, and remembering that the building was almost empty now, or at least assuming it was, he started to scream at the top of his lungs. After a bit, he started to feel it wasn't enough, so he went to the back bedroom, unlocked the door, crossed the floor, and flung the window wide. It was quiet out there, too, and he shouted and sang until the windows across the way opened and he could hear people cursing. He shouted abuse back. Something clattered against the window frame. He yelled a few more insults then slumped to the floor and sat beneath the sill, his back to the wall, waiting for someone to come knocking on his door. But no one did, so he drank some more. Then Sally was there.

How had she gotten into the apartment, he wanted to know, but his tongue was heavy in his mouth. Her palm was laid against his forehead and she was asking what he was doing to himself. Hadn't he decided to throw himself down the well of madness? Hadn't that helped?

He looked at her. She was sitting as she always used to, clasping her knees to her chest to make room for them both in the cell. She smiled. He loved that smile, even by the murky yellow glow that came through the little hatch high up on the door. His madness was beautiful, she said, all that greenery and music. Then she told him that Wagdi was fine, that he was abroad, that one day he would join him.

From a single point deep inside him, Warif felt a panic start to spread and grow, but then he felt a hand gripping that point and squeezing. What was left of his mind was scrambling to find connections between everything that was happening. There seemed to be someone in chains suspended from the ceiling of the little room, rattling in their chains; he didn't pity the person, he was frightened. He was frightened they'd get loose, and the next thing he knew the person, who looked like a zombie, had started to untangle themselves. As the zombie was getting loose, the door to the room swung open, so Warif began edging his way across the room, but then, all of a sudden, the zombie leaped free and landed on the floor in front of him.

Warif sat bolt upright and opened his eyes. His heart was a rubber ball bouncing around in his ribcage, but he struggled to his feet and staggered from the room. He went to the balcony that faced the Magra al-Uyoun aqueduct. With his eyes on the edge of the forest that spread toward Downtown, he drew in a deep gasping breath, slowly exhaled, and lowered himself to the cold tiles.

The platform at the top of the Muqattam cliff was higher than he had thought, than he could even have imagined. And they were right: there were no planes or paragliders in sight. Instead, something like a giant rubber catapult flung you high into the air over the rolling parkland, the parachute opened automatically, and you drifted down to land in the green expanse.

He'd signed a form saying that he'd received the necessary instructions, but he still felt nervous as he was being zipped into the safety suit and harness. A spring wind was blowing hard and some of the group had already backed out: Jalnoor said she wasn't heavy enough; Sally said she preferred to watch. But a few—Jakob, of course, among them—had tried it before and said they'd enjoyed it. Through the roaring of the wind at the cliff's edge, Warif could just make out his phone ringing. It was Souad; they hadn't spoken in days. He hesitated briefly then accepted the call:

"I'm fine," said Wagdi's voice.

Warif didn't know what to say; the words seemed to jumble in his mouth. Then Wagdi's voice came again, faint on the far end of the line. "I'm going to take it easy today. Come over tomorrow and I'll tell you everything."

It was the greatest surge of pure happiness that Warif had felt in longer than he cared to remember. He turned back to the platform with a grin. Sally wanted to know what had happened and he answered with a vague, "Great news…"

They positioned him on the catapult and winched him back. As he flew heavenward he found his lips moving, murmuring, "What I am doing?"

The wind gusted and he suddenly remembered how little he weighed now, barely half of what he used to. It was like being lifted on the palm of a vast, invisible hand. By now he should have reached the top of his arc and begun to fall, the parachute should be opening, but nothing seemed to be happening.

He looked down at the densely packed crowns

of the trees—maple and willow and fig and poplar—and was carried past them, still climbing. He thought he saw the gazelles lifting their heads to look at him. The grass seemed to stretch away forever. Then, in the distance, he glimpsed the line of the Nile and then the desert beyond it, and he said to himself that Wagdi would never believe everything you could see from up here.